"You want me to stay*** ***

Hannah asked, her brown eyes wide and wary.

"Don't look so shocked," Jeff said easily, giving her a reassuring smile. "I'm only suggesting you stay as my houseguest."

"You can't be serious." Nervously, she moistened her lips, and when she lowered her glass, her fingers trembled. "I can't stay here."

"Why not?"

"Why not?" Hannah repeated. "There's dozens of reasons."

"Name one."

"Jeff—" Her mind went blank. She couldn't think. Picking up her napkin, she twisted it into a tight ball as she frantically tried to come up with an answer. "For goodness' sake, you've got your own life to lead. I'd be in the way. Besides, we hardly know each other."

Jeff shook his head. "I feel like I've known you a long, long time...."

Dear Reader,

Welcome to Silhouette **Special Edition** . . . welcome to romance. Each month, Silhouette **Special Edition** publishes six novels with you in mind—stories of love and life, tales that you can identify with— romance with that little "something special" added in.

And this month is no exception to the rule—June 1991 brings *The Gauntlet* by Lindsay McKenna—the next thrilling WOMEN OF GLORY tale. Don't miss this story, or *Under Fire,* coming in July.

And to round out June, stories by Marie Ferrarella, Elizabeth Bevarly, Gina Ferris, Pat Warren and Sarah Temple are coming your way.

In each Silhouette **Special Edition,** we're dedicated to bringing you the romances that you dream about— the type of stories that delight as well as bring a tear to the eye. And that's what Silhouette **Special Edition** is all about—special books by special authors for special readers!

I hope that you enjoy this book and all the stories to come.

Sincerely,

Tara Gavin
Senior Editor

SARAH TEMPLE
Lifeline

Silhouette Special Edition

Published by Silhouette Books New York

America's Publisher of Contemporary Romance

To Robert and Ella Ruth Lanham,
the very best people and the very best parents

SILHOUETTE BOOKS
300 East 42nd St., New York, N.Y. 10017

LIFELINE

Copyright © 1991 by Cheryl Arguile

ISBN: 0-373-09674-7

First Silhouette Books printing June 1991

Printed in the U.S.A.

Books by Sarah Temple

Silhouette Special Edition

A Bouquet of Wildflowers #593
Lifeline #674

SARAH TEMPLE

Sarah Temple has been a jack-of-all-trades throughout her adult life. She worked her way through college as a waitress, motel maid and pool-hall clerk. Then she traveled to Europe and met her husband in England. For the past eight years, she has been employed by a Chinese steamship company, where she moved her way up to personnel manager.

Sarah says that the biggest influence on her writing has been other writers. She loves to read their stories, then dream up her own.

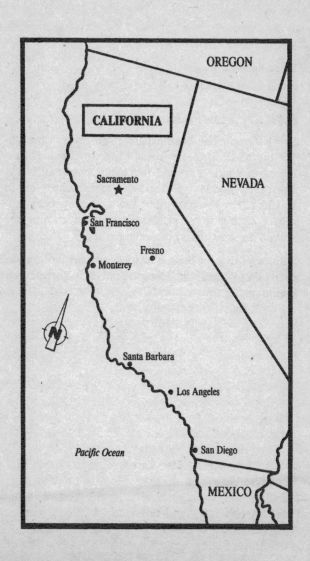

Chapter One

He knew it was her. Even without a picture or a description, the moment she'd pulled her car into the parking lot he'd known it was her.

Hannah Breckenridge.

He watched the tall auburn-haired woman slam the door of the compact and walk slowly toward a row of modern, Spanish-style apartments.

Jeff Kenyon took a deep breath as she climbed a short flight of steps and stopped in front of her door. He studied her carefully, wanting to learn as much as possible about her before he approached.

Her head was bent over her purse as she dug for her keys. She wasn't dressed casually, as you'd expect on a Sunday afternoon; instead she wore a narrow black skirt and a cream-colored sweater. He wondered where she'd been all day and decided it didn't matter. She was here now.

She opened her door and disappeared inside. Jeff tightened his grip on the steering wheel of the rental car to keep his hands from trembling. He'd never been this worried in his entire life. His nerves were as tight as a coiled spring. But then again, he reminded himself, nothing had ever been this important before.

Jeff lifted his fingers from the steering wheel and flexed them to force the rigid muscles to relax. He stared blindly at his hands, his mind's eye still seeing the look of relief on his father's face when they'd heard that Hannah Breckenridge had been located. He could still hear Reece's voice, uncharacteristically shaky, as he speculated whether perhaps they should send an attorney to meet with her first. But Jeff had nixed that idea.

He could understand his parents' worry; he was nervous, too. But he had the strongest feeling their best shot at success was with the personal approach. This wasn't a matter for a bunch of lawyers. There was too much at stake, too much to lose. It was *their* responsibility and *their* problem—Kirsten's problem.

His heart raced and he could hear the pulse pounding in his temples. Closing his eyes, he took another long breath to calm himself. He had to be in control. Rational. He didn't want her thinking he was some kind of nut case. This was too important to risk her slamming the door in his face before he could talk to her.

Jeff opened his eyes and glanced at her apartment. He got out of the car. His footsteps echoed loudly on the pavement, keeping time with the steady drumbeat of his heart. He repeated the vow he'd made before leaving San Francisco. No matter what it took, no matter what the cost, he'd make her understand. Kirsten was running out of time.

Hannah closed the door and dropped her purse on the end table. She crossed the room and sank down into the beige-and-white striped sofa. Yawning, she leaned her head back against the overstuffed cushions and smiled at the blissful solitude.

Her conscience nagged her to do her laundry, but she blithely ignored it. She was enjoying the peace and quiet too much to move. Besides, she told herself, she'd done her good deed for the day. Anyone who'd spent the afternoon fetching and carrying for the elderly ladies of St. John's Presbyterian Church deserved a rest. Who would have thought she'd get so exhausted from helping her mother run a bake sale? Hannah shook her head in amusement as she thought of the mountain of cookies she'd handled that afternoon. Those sweet little old ladies had made enough goodies to send an army battalion into a sugar coma. And they'd sold every last crumb.

Kicking her shoes off, Hannah lifted her feet onto the glass-topped coffee table. She sighed in relief as the image of her mother's sparkling eyes and excited chatter flashed through her mind. It was the first time in months she'd seen Mary acting like her old self. Hannah's tired feet and aching back were worth it.

The doorbell rang. She groaned and rose to answer the door, opening it a few inches. A tall blue-eyed man stared at her. She smiled politely and waited for him to speak.

He didn't say a word; he just looked at her.

"Can I help you?" she asked after a few seconds.

Jeff knew he should introduce himself, but he was so surprised he was speechless. He hadn't expected her to be so beautiful.

Beneath the curls of auburn hair piled on top of her head, her face was fine-boned and aristocratic. She had high cheekbones, a straight nose and a full, sensuous mouth.

Their gazes met and held. Then he smiled at the wary, puzzled look on her face. But it wasn't her expression that captivated him; it was the color of her eyes—deep, rich chocolate brown. A startling contrast against the pale ivory of her flawless skin.

He saw her face tighten in suspicion, and the urgency of his task came back to him in a quick rush. Damn, what was he doing?

"Miss Breckenridge?" he asked politely.

Hannah's eyes widened at the stranger who'd called her by name. "Yes," she admitted cautiously. "I'm Hannah Breckenridge. Who are you? One of my neighbors?"

"No," he replied quickly. "My name is Jeff Kenyon. I've come all the way from San Francisco to see you. It's very important. May I come in?"

"How did you know my name?" Hannah asked. She wasn't listed in the phone book nor was her name on the mailbox.

"Please don't be alarmed, Miss Breckenridge." His voice was soft, soothing. "I know who you are because I need to talk to you. You could say it's a matter of life and death."

Hannah relaxed a fraction but didn't open the door. She realized she had to tilt her head up to see him, and that wasn't particularly reassuring. He was a good half a head taller than her own five foot seven, and respectably dressed in a lightweight navy jacket, plaid shirt and pressed jeans. But one couldn't be too careful. North San Diego County wasn't the mean streets of Los Angeles, but he was still a perfect stranger.

"That's a bit melodramatic, isn't it?"

"No," he contradicted. "It isn't. I've come to see you about my sister, and it *is* urgent."

"All right, Mr. Kenyon. You can come in," she said. "But if you don't mind, I'll leave the front door open."

He cocked one dark eyebrow at that and she thought she saw the ghost of a grin on his mouth, but he made no comment.

Hannah remained standing beside the open door. She smiled tightly, not caring if he thought her behavior paranoid.

"Why don't you sit down and tell me what this is all about?" she said briskly, motioning him toward the sofa.

She studied him as he walked across the room and sat down. He was attractive. Not just tall, but sleekly muscled and lean. His hair was dark brown and had a hint of a wave. It was brushed away from his broad forehead and was long enough in the back to curl slightly over the collar of his jacket.

He glanced up at her and smiled. His eyes were a light sky-blue and framed by black lashes long enough to make most women green with envy. His eyebrows were thick and strongly arched. He had a sharp, square jawline softened by a rounded chin and a mouth that looked as though it smiled a lot. From the lines etched around his eyes and lips, Hannah estimated he was in his mid-thirties.

"Miss Breckenridge," he said, sitting forward and clasping his hands between his knees. "I wasn't joking when I said I've come about a matter of life and death."

She crossed her arms in front of her. "I believe you mentioned a sister."

He looked down at his hands and then back up at Hannah. "My sister's name is Kirsten Kenyon, and she's in a lot of trouble."

So that's it, thought Hannah, relaxing. The mystery was over. Of course, it was so simple she felt a little foolish for not having guessed right away. But it was a bit unusual for one of the community center's clients to come to see her directly. After all, she was an administrator, not a counselor. *Kirsten Kenyon.* Hannah frowned and shook her head. She couldn't place the girl.

"I'm afraid I don't recall your sister," Hannah told him apologetically. "But we have hundreds of clients at the center. Which program is she in?"

Jeff looked puzzled. "She's not in any program. Kirsten doesn't live in San Diego and she's never been to your center."

"You don't have to live in the area," she explained hastily. "The Inner-City Community Center serves anyone in need. We're not government sponsored so there are no residency requirements." Hannah moved away from the wall. "Let me give you one of my cards. I'm an administrator down there, but if your sister's in trouble I can refer her to—"

"I'm afraid you don't understand," Jeff interrupted. "I didn't come here to ask you to get her into any kind of program. Kirsten doesn't need counseling for emotional problems or an unwanted pregnancy."

He stopped and ran his hand through his hair. "God," he said softly, closing his eyes. "I wish it were that simple."

Confused, she stared at him.

"I'm not here to see you in your professional capacity," he continued, gazing up at her. "Kirsten does need help—a kind of help that I'm praying you *can* and *will* give."

Hannah shifted uneasily at his words. "You'd better be a little more specific. Exactly what are you asking for?"

Jeff straightened and gave her a long, level stare. "Kirsten has leukemia," he answered, his voice sounding unnaturally loud in the quiet apartment. "She needs a bone-marrow transplant."

Every muscle in Hannah's body tensed. She didn't want to ask any more questions, but she had to. "And what does that have to do with me?"

Jeff leaned forward, watching her intently and choosing his next words with care. "We have reason to believe your tissue might be compatible with my sister's. I'm asking you to take a blood test. If you're a match, we'll pay you anything to be a donor for Kirsten."

Stunned, Hannah could only stare at him. After all these years it was happening. She suspected she knew why he'd come to her, but suspicion wasn't fact.

"Mr. Kenyon," she asked somberly, "what on earth would make you think I might be compatible with your sister?"

Her heart was pounding so loudly now, she was sure he could hear it; and it took every ounce of willpower she possessed to keep her voice from shaking. She'd waited for this moment all her life. Waited and dreaded and wanted and hoped for.

"She's your half sister," he replied softly, his gaze locked on her face. "You're an adoptee. You're one of my sister's living blood relatives. That's why we're praying you might be compatible."

Jeff knew his words had astounded her. He watched her turn pale, saw her muscles tense and her body go rigid. A look of overwhelming disbelief appeared on her face. Alarmed, he leaped to his feet and crossed to where she stood.

"Are you all right?" he asked, his voice full of concern. "Are you going to faint? Do you want me to get you something? A glass of water..."

She gazed up and saw his worry. She tried to smile. "No, I'm all right. I'm sorry," she murmured shakily. "I didn't mean to scare you. But this is quite a shock."

"No," he countered earnestly. "Please don't apologize. I'm the one who's sorry. But there wasn't really any gentle way to break the news, and my sister is running out of time. I had to come. Kirsten needs a transplant now. It's the only thing that might save her life, and you're our last hope."

Hannah shook herself and stepped back. She took a deep breath of air and walked over to stare out the window. Her hands were trembling so, she clasped them tightly together in front of her. She tried to think, to understand what was happening. But no coherent thought passed through her mind.

"I didn't even know I had a sister," she finally said.

Jeff was at a loss how to proceed. He'd known she'd be surprised at his request. But he hadn't bargained on her extreme reaction. Everything had seemed so simple before he left San Francisco.

His mission had been to find Hannah Breckenridge and ask her to help. But it wasn't working out like that. She was clearly stunned, and he didn't have a clue what to do or say next.

Was it possible she hadn't known she was adopted? His eyes narrowed at that horrifying possibility and he swore silently. Damn! He didn't want to upset her anymore, but he needed an answer now.

"Hannah," he said gently, "please forgive me for blurting it out the way I did. I'm usually more diplomatic than that. But I assumed you knew you were adopted."

"I knew I was adopted," she whispered. "I just didn't know I had a sister."

Adopted. Such a precise word, Hannah reflected dazedly. There was nothing vague or uncertain about its meaning. You knew exactly what the word meant. It meant your own mother had given you away. Refusing to give in to self-pity, she took a long, calming breath of air and stared blindly at the fading California sunshine. The reasons you were given away didn't matter; they were generally excellent reasons. But there was always that one small part of you that cringed every time you heard that word.

Adopted.

Hannah stiffened her spine and got herself under control. She'd come to terms with being adopted years ago. She hoped to God her sister had, too.

Jeff cleared his throat, bringing Hannah back to the present. She turned and gave him a strained smile. He watched her closely, his expression concerned.

Kirsten was lucky, Hannah thought, just as she had been. The Kenyon family obviously loved their adopted daughter very much.

"I don't know how you found me," she said, "but it really doesn't matter right now. I'll do whatever I can to help Kirsten."

Relief, swift and potent, flooded Jeff's whole body. He expelled the breath he'd been holding and closed his eyes, sending up a small prayer of thanks that Hannah Breckenridge was a decent person. "Thank you," he muttered hoarsely. "You were our last hope."

He gave her a brilliant smile—the kind of smile that could have sent her heart jackhammering if she hadn't seen the gratitude in those beautiful blue eyes.

Gratitude. Such a strong emotion, she thought fleetingly. An emotion far more powerful than most people understood it to be. But *she* understood it.

Hannah felt numb, as if this conversation were happening to someone else. She blinked as she realized he was waiting for her to say something.

A gust of winter wind blew through the open door, rattling the newspapers on the end table. Hannah gave Jeff a brief smile and quickly walked across the room.

"Would you like some coffee, Mr. Kenyon?" she called as she closed the door. Deliberately Hannah kept her back to him. She didn't want to have to look at his expression anymore.

Gratitude. One of the most painful and terrifying of all emotions. But he couldn't understand that. No one did.

"As you can imagine," she continued, "I've got lots of questions."

"I'd love some coffee, and please call me Jeff."

She nodded briskly and went to the kitchen. Jeff sat down on the couch again and gazed around her apartment. The place was nice, very nice. But then so was the woman who lived here. He looked down at the light hardwood floors and stared at his shoes.

He grinned as he realized his luck was holding. He'd not only found her, he'd gotten her to cooperate. The moment she'd realized a life was at stake, she'd agreed to help.

Hannah Breckenridge, he decided, was one very special lady. *And a beautiful one.* He sobered instantly and then shrugged. Her looks weren't important, he told himself. All that mattered was getting her to take the blood test.

His gaze swept the apartment and he noticed a picture on the bookcase by the front door. Quietly he rose to his feet and crossed the room. He stood for a moment staring at an oak-framed photograph of Hannah and two other people. Smiling slightly, he picked up the picture and studied it. A silver-haired man wearing a clerical collar, an attractive middle-aged blond woman and Hannah smiled back at him. Her parents, he surmised. Jeff heard the clink of china from the kitchen. He put the picture back where he'd found it and turned. Hannah was putting cups and saucers on a tray.

Frowning, Jeff moved back to the couch. The photo had reminded him of his stepmother. Irene. Damn. He glanced at Hannah again and knew he couldn't bring himself to broach the subject. She'd had enough shocks for one day. Irene would just have to wait—at least until they knew whether or not Hannah could be a donor.

A moment later, Hannah returned carrying a tray of coffee. She set it on the table and poured two cups. Handing one to Jeff, she sat down across from him and murmured, "Help yourself to cream and sugar."

Jeff reached for the sugar bowl. "Why don't we get started on those questions of yours?" he suggested, striving to keep his voice casual.

Hannah took a sip of coffee. "How old is Kirsten?"

"She's seventeen."

"Does she live with you?"

"She lives in Alameda with my parents. I live up there, too. Not with my parents, of course." Jeff smiled. "I have an apartment in San Francisco. My folks live on the east side of the bay. We own a transportation company in Oakland. Kenyon International."

"Oh, yes," Hannah replied. She was relieved to move on to a mundane topic. "I've seen some trucks on the freeway with that name." She broke off suddenly as it hit her that a normal conversation wasn't possible. This was too abnormal a situation.

"How long has Kirsten been ill?" she asked softly.

"She was diagnosed two years ago." Jeff put his cup down. "Can you get time off from work tomorrow to take the blood test? We really are running out of time."

She stared at Jeff, her eyes filled with compassion. "And if I'm not compatible?" she ventured soberly. "What then? Are there other treatments? Is there anything else that can be done?"

Jeff looked down at the floor for a moment and then raised his gaze to meet hers. His eyes were bleak and filled with agony.

"I'm sorry," she said quickly. "I shouldn't have asked that." She stopped and drew a breath. "But in answer to your original question, there shouldn't be any problem getting time off tomorrow. My employers at the community center are a group of churches and synagogues." Hannah smiled and forced her voice to a lightness she didn't feel. "They're a pretty compassionate bunch down there. They'll give me all the time I need."

Some of the bleakness left Jeff's face. "That's good. We'll try not to disrupt your life too much, but as you can imagine, the logistics of the situation can get complicated."

"Exactly what will this entail?" Hannah asked, curious. She tilted her head. "What do I need to do?"

"The first thing is to have the blood test. Everything hinges on that. It will show whether or not your tissue is compatible with Kirsten's."

"Just from a blood test?" She was surprised it was that simple.

Jeff nodded. "I've made you an appointment for eleven tomorrow morning at a clinic near Mission Bay."

She laughed. "You must have been pretty sure of me."

"Not really," he replied, breaking into a grin. "But I had a feeling you'd say yes and I wanted to have everything arranged just in case."

"And then what happens?"

"If the blood tests show tissue compatibility, we'd need you to fly to San Francisco for the transplant procedure." Jeff hesitated. "You'd probably have to be up there for a couple of weeks. Would that be a problem?"

Hannah shook her head. "No. In a case like this, I can get as much time off as I need."

He leaned back and gave her a long, thoughtful stare. "I'm not just talking about your job. Most people generally have other responsibilities in their life—other people who have a claim on them, who might object if they were suddenly gone for two weeks."

Hannah took a sip of coffee, staring at him over the rim of her cup, her expression puzzled.

"I'm talking about a boyfriend or a fiancé," Jeff explained hastily.

Her answer was suddenly important to him. He didn't know why, and the question hadn't entered his mind until now. But he was curious to know if Hannah was involved with a man. At the same time, he was irritated with himself for wanting to know.

"If I'm not worried about my employers' objecting to my being gone," Hannah pointed out, "I'm certainly not going to worry about anyone else's objections. You did say a life was at stake here."

It was both the truth and a lie. There *was* someone Hannah worried about. But she'd think about that later. She couldn't handle it now.

"Tell me about Kirsten's illness," she commanded gently. "I thought leukemia was treated with chemotherapy and radiation."

"It is. As a matter of fact, both those methods have helped Kirsten stay alive. But the doctors say her best chance for a cure is a transplant now, while she's in partial remission. When they told us that, everyone in the family was tested for compatibility. But that was a dead end. None of us matched. We put all the particulars about Kirsten onto the National Marrow Donor Program, but there are too few donors for that to be of much hope. So I came searching for you.'' He looked her straight in the eye. ''And thank God, you were easy to find and you're willing to help.''

Hannah was confused. Why would the Kenyons have tested? Surely the odds of one of them being a match with an adopted daughter were pretty remote?

She started to ask and then realized it was a foolish question. Naturally they'd tested. If the situation had been reversed, if it were her fighting a deadly disease, her parents would have done the same thing. No matter how poor the odds, her family would have tried. Any family would.

They sipped their coffee in silence for a few moments. Hannah was grateful for the reprieve. She needed the time to get her reeling emotions in order.

She had a sister. A blood relative. A link with another living person that wasn't forged through circumstances, but by blood. It was a heady thought, a cherished dream; a forbidden delight that seeped into her body and washed deliciously through her bones.

Seconds later, her mother's face flashed across her consciousness and she felt guilty. Hannah drew herself up. ''How did you find me?'' she asked curiously. ''My adoption records were sealed when I was born.''

Jeff didn't answer. He drummed his fingers on the tabletop and looked everywhere but at Hannah. Finally he raised his eyes to meet hers. ''We hired a detective.''

She frowned. ''A detective? But I don't see how—''

"He cut a few corners," Jeff interjected. He straightened and gave her a long, appraising stare. "I instructed the agency to do whatever was necessary to find you. We were, after all, desperate."

Amazed, Hannah slumped against the cushions. Jeff no longer looked embarrassed. Any discomfort he might have felt was gone; his face looked hard and determined and completely unrepentant.

"Exactly what did your detective have to do?"

"Adoption records can be obtained, even sealed ones."

A brief spurt of anger flared in Hannah. "You illegally broke into my adoption records?"

"Yes," he admitted honestly. "Like I said, we were desperate. Look, I know you probably feel we've violated your privacy. But the only thing we did was track down your current address by using the names and occupations of your parents. That's all. I promise you, we didn't go snooping around in your private life." If we had, he thought, I'd know whether or not there was a boyfriend in the picture.

Torn between anger and understanding, Hannah stared at him. He looked right back at her, his expression implacable and utterly honest. She believed him.

Her anger evaporated as quickly as it had come. Jeff Kenyon was obviously the kind of man who would do whatever it took to help someone he loved.

"I see," she replied. "But what I don't understand is how you even knew I existed. There's a big age gap between Kirsten and me. I'm twenty-nine, she's seventeen. That's twelve years. How did you even know to look for me? How did you know I existed? I mean, we might both be adopted, but—" Flustered, she broke off as she watched the expression on his face change from polite interest to complete incredulity.

Jeff was reaching for his coffee. He stopped, his cup halfway to his mouth. Without thinking, he said, "Kirsten isn't adopted."

Chapter Two

"What did you say?" Hannah was sure she'd misunderstood him. Of course Kirsten was adopted. She had to be.

Jeff carefully set his coffee cup on the table before answering. He looked at Hannah, his expression hesitant. "I said," he repeated slowly, "Kirsten isn't adopted. She's my half-sister. We have the same father."

Hannah stared at him blankly. She heard herself continuing the conversation as though it were the most normal thing in the world.

"But you said I was Kirsten's only living relative."

Jeff shook his head. "You must have misunderstood," he told her gently. "I said you were *one* of Kirsten's living relatives. My dad and I both tested for compatibility," he explained quickly, "but we weren't a match, and the doctors wouldn't let Irene test because she picked up a bad case of hepatitis last year in Hong Kong."

"I take it Irene is Kirsten's mother." Her voice sounded unusually controlled, even to herself.

"Yes," Jeff answered cautiously, his eyes never leaving hers. She sounded calm and composed now. He heaved a sigh of relief.

"But Irene isn't your mother?" Robotlike, her questions kept coming.

The tone of her voice bothered him. Jeff sat back and studied her. His eyes narrowed with concern as his gaze swept her and he realized what lay beneath that poised exterior.

She sat perfectly still. Her arms were crossed defensively, her face was pale, and in her eyes there was a fear bordering on panic.

Hannah was as easy to read as a road map.

He couldn't do it; he couldn't subject her to any more stress. Jeff didn't know whether he was acting to protect her or to ensure that she cooperated with them. All he knew was, he didn't want Hannah suffering any further trauma tonight because of the Kenyons. Tomorrow would be soon enough.

"Look," he went on reasonably, "why don't we leave the explanations till later? I'm sorry I let that slip about Kirsten. I'll explain everything tomorrow."

"Let it slip?" she echoed incredulously, shaking her head. "What do you mean by that? Were you trying to hide something from me? Admittedly this has all been rather startling, but I assure you, I'd much rather know the truth now instead of later."

Hannah knew she wouldn't sleep a wink all night unless Jeff told her everything. However upsetting the truth was, it was better to get it out in the open. She'd faced hard news before; she could do it again.

"I've told you the truth," Jeff stated flatly.

She raised an eyebrow and then shrugged. "Maybe you have. But it's pretty obvious I've made a lot of incorrect assumptions. I assumed you came looking for me because Kirsten was an adoptee, too. I assumed that's why none of your family was compatible and that's why you needed me as a possible donor." She paused, closed her eyes for a moment and then smiled wryly. "I guess I assumed a little too much."

Jeff sighed. "I'm sorry you got that impression. I wasn't deliberately trying to hide anything."

"If Kirsten isn't adopted," she interjected, "does that mean you're my brother?"

"No," Jeff exclaimed loudly. Too loudly. Her brother? "No," he repeated, lowering his voice. "I'm not your brother."

His reaction to her question was immediate and instinctively male. Despite the importance of his reason for being here, having met her, he was damned sure he didn't want her developing any *brotherly* ideas about him.

She tilted her head and raised her chin, looking both confused and determined at the same time. "I'm Kirsten's sister and you're Kirsten's brother, but you're not my brother?"

"Let me explain." He took a deep breath. This was the tough part. He'd hoped it could wait till later, till she was committed to helping. "My mother died when I was seven. I was an only child and for years it was just Dad and me. When I was fourteen, my father met and fell in love with Irene. They were married a few

months later. Two years after that, Kirsten was born.''
Jeff broke off and looked away.

"Go on," Hannah urged, wanting—no—needing
for him to spell it out for her.

Jeff turned and met her gaze. His blue eyes were
filled with compassion. "Irene's your mother."

She drew back and stared at him, not saying a word.
Her face went completely blank. In that moment, he'd
have given a lot to be able to read minds. He felt the
silence tighten and stretch like a length of wire being
pulled across his throat.

"I see," she finally responded. She looked down at
her hands. For years she'd had a secret, guilty fantasy
that one day she'd learn who her natural mother was;
she'd find her roots, be part of a blood tie, know what
nationality she'd come from. It was a dream she'd
never dared express to anyone, especially to her
adoptive mother. But now this stranger was sitting in
her living room, calmly giving her the knowledge she'd
craved for years, and she didn't feel one damned thing.
Absolutely nothing.

"Hannah," Jeff said softly.

"No wonder it was so easy for you to find me," she
remarked thoughtfully. "Obviously she could tell you
exactly what you needed to know, where to start
looking."

Jeff watched her with troubled eyes. "I'm sorry.
This is a lousy way for you to find out about your
mother."

She raised her head sharply, but when she looked at
him her eyes were glazed and unfocused. Hannah
wanted to scream at him that this Irene person wasn't
her mother; she was only a biological fact that Han-

nah had stopped thinking about years ago. Her mother was Mary Breckenridge.

"Don't worry about it," she muttered, staring off into the distance.

Her brain seemed to split in two. One half was frantically working on the ramifications of what Jeff had just told her, while the other half was busily sealing her emotions into a tight little corner—a corner she'd deal with later, when she was alone.

Irene Kenyon, her natural mother... Dear God, she thought, this changes everything! An image of Mary's face flashed before her eyes and she swallowed. What on earth was she going to do? A sister was one thing, but a *birth mother* ... Hannah shivered. She knew Mary couldn't handle that.

"Does this change anything?" Jeff's question uncannily echoed her thoughts.

With an effort, she forced herself to look at him.

"Will you still help us? Will you still take the blood test?" he pressed anxiously. He hated asking her again, but instinctively he'd known that somehow everything had been altered. Her very lack of response was a bad sign. Oh, hell, he thought dismally. Maybe he should have left this up to the lawyers.

"Of course, I'll still help." Hannah rose to her feet and faced him. "But I hadn't realized the situation was quite this complicated."

Jeff watched her apprehensively. All the warmth had faded from those beautiful brown eyes and her face was closed and taut. When she spoke, her tone was cold and impersonal.

"I'm still willing to take the blood test," she said firmly. "But I'm afraid there'll have to be a few ground rules now."

His mouth went dry. "What kind of rules?"

"I'll have to insist that no one in your family has any contact with me."

Jeff exhaled the breath he'd been holding. He'd agree to anything as long as she wasn't changing her mind about taking the blood test. He thought of Irene and winced inwardly. This could be a problem. But he'd deal with it later. Now wasn't the time to start campaigning for anything except getting Hannah to that clinic tomorrow. "And exactly what does that mean?"

"It means precisely what I said. I don't want any of my—my—" she stumbled over the words "—birth relatives making contact with me. Not for any reason whatsoever."

She stared at him defiantly, as though challenging him to argue. Jeff was surprised by her reaction. He didn't know what he'd expected. Curiosity, maybe. Or a few tears. He'd even been prepared for an outburst of bitterness and resentment that she'd been given up for adoption. But he wasn't prepared for this apparent lack of curiosity or feeling.

The rough world he worked in had taught him how to hide his feelings when the situation called for it. And the situation definitely called for it now. He couldn't risk offending Hannah.

"May I ask why?" He forced himself to smile politely.

"I'm sorry." She hesitated and her look of cold defiance faded. For a split second her eyes filled with anguish but she quickly lowered her lashes. "I'd rather not go into it. Let's just say I have my reasons, and leave it at that."

Hannah knew she sounded evasive. She didn't want to, but she wasn't going to tell him about Mary. Her mother's inability to cope with birth families was a personal matter—not something to be discussed with a stranger.

Hannah looked Jeff squarely in the eye. "Do you understand what I'm saying? There's to be no contact whatsoever between your family and me. Is that clear?"

"Very." His face hardened a fraction. He rose to his feet, reached into the pocket of his jacket and drew out a slip of paper. Handing it to her, he said, "Here's the address of the clinic. Please, don't forget it's at eleven o'clock tomorrow morning."

"Thanks." She glanced briefly at the paper before putting it into her purse. She was aware of Jeff staring curiously at her back. She didn't care. Let him think what he liked, let him believe she was a selfish, unforgiving witch. It didn't matter. She knew he'd accept her help.

The one important thing was to make sure Mary didn't get hurt.

Her mother was now just finally getting over the grief of her husband's death, and Hannah wasn't about to let anything interfere with that. That Hannah had a sister, Mary could handle. But a birth mother? No. That would be too much.

Hannah dug out one of her business cards and handed it to Jeff. "Here's my number at work. Call me if there's any other information you need to give me."

He glanced briefly at her card and stuffed it into his pocket. From across the coffee table, they stared at each other. He knew she wanted him to go, but he couldn't force himself to walk to the front door. He didn't want to leave.

Hannah was intriguing and fascinating. Vulnerable one minute and then cold as ice the next. Under any other circumstances, he knew he'd be very attracted to her.

For a moment, he wished they'd met in another time and another place. Jeff stared at the inviting shape of her mouth and let himself imagine how she'd taste. His body began to respond and the real reason he was standing in Hannah's apartment came flooding back. Quickly he shifted his weight and looked away, disgusted with himself for reacting so strongly to her—especially under these appalling circumstances.

She watched him coolly, her expression one of polite disinterest. Pointedly Hannah glanced at the door, and Jeff decided not to push any further.

"This has all come as a shock to you," he sympathized, wanting somehow to placate her. He also wanted her to know how much her cooperation meant to his family.

The hardness had left his face but Hannah hated the expression that replaced it. She knew what he was going to say before he finished his sentence.

"I want you to know how grateful we are."

"It's all right," she cut in quickly, unwilling to hear any more. "Please don't thank me. Any decent person would try to help."

Hannah walked purposefully toward the door. She wanted Jeff Kenyon to take his gratitude and leave her in peace. His footsteps echoed faintly on the hardwood floor as he followed her. She pulled the door open and turned. He was standing right behind her, watching her with a thoughtful expression.

Their eyes met for an instant, then he nodded abruptly and stepped past her. In the doorway he stopped and said, "I'll call you tomorrow to see how things went with the test. Is that all right?"

"That's fine," she muttered with a tiny smile.

They said goodbye and Hannah watched him walk across the parking lot toward his car. She closed the door and collapsed against it.

Back at his hotel, Jeff picked up the phone and dialed his parents' house in Alameda.

Reece Kenyon answered on the first ring. "Hello. Jeff, is that you?"

"It's me, Dad." He didn't waste a moment telling them the news. "She's going to take the blood test tomorrow. If she's a match, she's agreed to be a donor."

"Thank God." Reece's voice was trembling with relief. "We've been on pins and needles all day. Irene's walked a hole in the carpet." He broke off and Jeff could hear him relaying the news to Irene. A moment later, his stepmother came on the line.

"Jeff. Oh, thank God. You did it. I told Reece you were right, all along. This was much too important to leave to our lawyers. I knew you'd find her. I knew you'd get her to help us." Irene paused and drew a shaky breath. "What's she like?" she asked softly.

"Hannah's very nice," he replied gently, "and as beautiful as you are. But there isn't any resemblance between the two of you."

Irene laughed and sniffed at the same time. "She must have asked a million questions. My God, this must have been a shock for her. I bet she was curious about all of us...." Her voice faltered. "Did she ask anything about me?"

"There wasn't time for her to ask much of anything," he answered quickly, hearing the silent plea in Irene's voice. "You were right, this was a shock for Hannah. I don't think she quite took it all in."

There was a long pause before Irene said, "I see."

"Irene..."

"I can't wait to meet her," she blurted out in a thick voice. "And to think she might be the one who helps save our baby—" Irene broke off and Jeff could hear her crying quietly. His gut twisted in pain.

Reece came back on the line. "Irene's a little emotional here."

"I understand," Jeff replied. "Dad, look, there may be a problem. Don't ask any questions. I don't want to upset Irene any more than she already is."

"All right," Reece answered lightly, indicating he'd understood his son's warning.

Jeff thought of Hannah's insistence on the Kenyons' staying away from her. Irene had to be warned, and his father was the only one capable of handling that.

"You'd better have a talk with Irene. Try and prepare her a little. Hannah's a stranger to us. She may need some time before she feels ready to meet her mother." He paused. "For that matter, there's a good chance she'll never want to meet Irene."

There was a moment's silence before Reece responded, "I understand." His tone was casual but Jeff knew his father had received his message. "I think I'm going to make Irene take one of those pills the doctor prescribed. None of us have had much sleep the past few days. Don't worry about us. We'll do just fine. I'll handle everything at this end."

"How's Kirsten doing today?"

"As well as can be expected," Reece replied somberly. "The isolation is getting to her, but she's coping."

"Did you tell her about Hannah?"

"No. We didn't want to get her hopes up. You remember what the doctor said—the odds of Hannah Breckenridge being a compatible match are pretty slim. We'll tell Kirsten after we know the test results."

Jeff closed his eyes and slumped against the wall. His beautiful seventeen-year-old sister was being kept in a sterile room the size of a broom closet. She was in constant pain and dosed frequently with blood transfusions, chemotherapy and antibiotics. And even now, when there was a glimmer of hope on the horizon, they couldn't say a word. Because Hannah might not be a match.

"I'll call you tomorrow," Jeff continued, swallowing his fears. "The clinic's been instructed to analyze the test ASAP, so we should know by the end of the week. Give my love to Kirsten."

Jeff hung up the phone and walked to the window. He stared out at the brilliant sunset bathing Mission Bay. But he was oblivious to the gorgeous view. Damn! he thought angrily, thinking of Hannah's terms for helping and what it would do to Irene. Just what we need—another problem.

There were no guarantees about Kirsten. He knew it, his parents knew it and soon, Hannah would know it. Would that change her mind? When she knew exactly what the odds were, would she soften her stance and agree to meet Kirsten and Irene? He thought again of the doctors' assessment of his sister's chances and sighed wearily.

Maybe it wouldn't make any difference to Hannah. She was definitely a puzzle. He frowned as he remembered those last moments in her apartment. One second she'd been so soft, and an instant later, she'd gone brittle as glass. Hell, she hadn't even wanted to let him say thanks.

He turned and gazed morosely around the luxurious hotel room before moving slowly to the bed. Kicking off his shoes he lay down and studied the ceiling. He should be feeling good. Hannah had agreed to take the test and even with the lousy odds, there was still hope. But as one part of him rejoiced at this chance for his sister, he couldn't help feeling guilty. He knew what they were doing to Hannah. She wasn't really hard; her willingness to help had been proof of that. And deep in his gut he knew exactly what his visit had done to her: it had devastated her.

He'd intruded into the life of a perfect stranger—an innocent woman who'd had her whole world turned upside down in the space of half an hour. And the worst part of it was, he'd do it again in a minute. No matter how much pain it caused Hannah Breckenridge.

In the distance a car backfired and the sound startled Hannah into moving. Mechanically she walked to the low table and loaded the coffee things onto the tray.

She put the cups and saucers in the sink and turned on the hot water. Glancing up, she caught her reflection in the decorative mirror under the window.

Why? a tiny voice she hadn't heard in years whispered from the back of her mind. Hannah didn't have the strength to fight the voice. Her emotions were too raw and her nerves too close to the surface. She could only stand and stare at the shadows on her face as the merciless questions hammered her relentlessly.

Why didn't she *love* me? Why didn't she *want* me? Why did she give *me* up? Why wasn't I good enough? Why? Why? Why?

"Ouch—" Hannah snatched her hand away from the now scalding spray of water. She frowned at her reddened fingers. This was ridiculous. What was wrong with her?

Disgusted, she turned off the spigot and grabbed a dish towel from under the sink. She hadn't indulged in this kind of adolescent self-pity in years.

For God's sake, she told herself sternly, working at the community center had shown her that the act of giving birth didn't automatically make someone mother material.

Hannah shrugged. She'd come to terms with being adopted when she was a teenager. She was just reacting to Jeff's visit, that's all. There were probably some very good reasons her birth mother had given her up— reasons that had nothing to do with her and everything to do with Irene Kenyon's circumstances twenty-nine years ago.

She put the sugar bowl back in the cupboard and switched off the coffeepot. Her expression grew thoughtful as she finished clearing up. This would cause problems. There was no getting around that. Her mother was irrational about birth families; that was a fact.

Determined to be logical about the situation, Hannah went into the living room and sat down on the couch. There had to be a way of telling Mary the truth without sending her straight back into a deep depression.

Her mother was far too good a person to deliberately make her feel guilty about helping Kirsten Kenyon. But Mary was so vulnerable right now—she might not be able to help herself. Hannah glanced at the family picture on the bookcase and smiled sadly. They were both vulnerable now.

Her father's death fourteen months ago had been hard on both of them. But Mary's grief had been overwhelming, plunging her into a black hole of depression she was just now climbing out of.

Hannah sighed. No, her mother would tell her to do everything possible to save a human life. But at the same time, she knew how much agony any contact between Hannah and her birth family would cause Mary.

She dragged her gaze away from the picture as memories from long ago drifted into her mind. Tears welled in her eyes as she recalled that awful day—the day they'd taken the baby away.

She could still hear her father's voice, trembling with emotion as he'd grabbed Mary to prevent her from tearing down the street after the social worker's disappearing car.

Hannah had been five at the time. She remembered the confusion and pain of knowing something terrible had happened to them, but not understanding exactly what it meant when her father had tried to explain that the baby's birth mother had changed her mind. Her six-month-old sister wasn't going to live with them anymore.

"But, Daddy," she'd sobbed, "how can she change her mind? Hope belongs to us. She's our baby. Why is that lady taking her? Make her bring her back, Daddy. Make her bring Hope back."

The Reverend Sam Breckenridge had lost control then, and started to cry himself. He hadn't tried to explain further, he'd just taken Hannah in his arms and held her tightly.

Mary had been a basket case for months after that. She'd hovered so closely over Hannah that her father had threatened to make her seek psychiatric help. When Mary realized the extent of her husband's worry, she'd made herself snap out of it and get on with her life.

But Mary had never gotten over her fear of losing the adopted daughter she had left.

She became neurotic about birth families. Mary couldn't even stand to read those poignant stories in the newspapers—the ones about adopted children finding and reuniting with their natural mothers. Those articles upset her so much that Sam and Hannah had taken to hiding every newspaper and magazine that came into the house if they spotted anything written about adoption.

Wearily Hannah slumped back against the cushions. She'd never make Jeff Kenyon understand. But that didn't matter. He didn't need to. She glanced over at the spot where he'd been sitting and smiled bitterly. No, he didn't need to understand. He'd be too *grateful.*

Gratitude. She shuddered. She hated that word, that emotion. She remembered the look on Jeff's face. It reminded her painfully of the last time she'd seen that expression on a man's face. Another shudder racked her body as she thought of the disaster her relationship with Kevin had turned into.

When she realized what she was thinking, she straightened abruptly and gasped out loud. Good Lord, what on earth was she doing? Comparing this situation to what had happened with Kevin was absurd. She'd been in love with Kevin but she scarcely knew Jeff.

Hannah shook her head. No, she told herself. Don't be ridiculous. It isn't the same. You're not even involved with the man. You don't even know him. Once you take the blood test, you'll never see Jeff Kenyon again. Even if you end up in San Francisco as a donor, there won't be any reason to see him. From this point on, everything will be done by phone. The situation's entirely different.

But was it?

Hannah chased the silly idea out of her head. Of course, Jeff was an attractive man; handsome, even. But she wasn't attracted to him. So why was she comparing him to Kevin?

Determined to ignore her outrageous thoughts, she leaped from the couch and headed grimly for a stack of paperwork she'd brought home to work on.

Nevertheless, the last thought drifting through Hannah's mind that night before she fell asleep was that this time she knew. This time she'd never mistake gratitude for anything but what it was.

She'd done that number before.

Chapter Three

Jeff rested his hands on his hips and stared at the huge battle-scarred building that housed the Inner-City Community Center. The windows were covered with heavy black security bars, graffiti in three different languages were plastered on the walls and the entrance was crowded with the kind of people who'd make the macho dockworkers at Kenyon International turn pale.

Jeff looked around slowly, shaking his head. Across the street, two dark-haired children played a make-shift game of handball against the dumpster in the unpaved parking lot of The Blue Fox Mexican Cantina. Mariachi music drifted through the open door of the bar and blended with the roar of cars and the low rumble of heavy trucks from the traffic on the busy street.

This was the place, all right. And it was in one of the roughest neighborhoods he'd ever seen. Worse, even, than the part of Oakland where the Kenyon warehouse was located.

A surge of admiration gripped him as he thought of Hannah. Her airy apartment flashed vividly into his mind—the modern oak furniture, the books and magazines, the elegant way she'd served him coffee and the vase filled with fresh flowers on the kitchen table.

Whatever misgivings he'd had about the wisdom of coming here disappeared. He wouldn't have missed seeing where she worked for anything. It told him everything he needed to know about her character.

Good God! he thought, as a filthy, disheveled man stumbled drunkenly out of the alley on the other side of the cantina, the woman had guts. Working in this neighborhood must be like taking your life in your hands every single day.

Jeff dropped his hands from his hips and started for the door.

Hannah tapped her pencil absently against her desk and glanced at the grant proposal she'd been working on since seven a.m. For once, she was grateful it had to be done in time to catch the evening mail. Completing the complex report had forced her to stop thinking about Jeff Kenyon and his surprise visit yesterday.

She picked up her pencil and erased the tiny note she'd made in the margin. There was a knock on her door and without even looking up, she called "Come in."

Jeff opened the door, leaned casually against the frame and stared at her. Her head was bent over her desk, and her face wore the deep, absorbed frown of concentration. That long auburn hair he'd been itching to touch was worn in a neat, businesslike twist on the top of her head and she was unconsciously tapping her pencil on the desktop.

Hannah glanced up and her eyes widened in surprise when she saw him. He wasn't smiling. As a matter of fact, she realized quickly, dropping the pencil, he was looking at her with a guarded, almost hesitant expression.

Her pulse quickened and her heartbeat accelerated as she stared wordlessly at her unexpected visitor. "What are you doing here?" she finally managed to gasp, her voice breathless.

"I could say I just happened to be in the neighborhood," he replied lightly. "But frankly, no one in their right mind would just happen to be in this neighborhood." He shoved away from the door and stepped into the room. "Not if they valued their hides."

Flustered by the contradiction between the teasing gleam in his eyes and his actual words, Hannah automatically gave him a reassuring smile. "It's not as bad as it looks," she said with a laugh. "But you do have to take precautions. Especially at night."

Why on earth was he here? And why was her heart pounding in her chest? Annoyed at her reaction to him, she drew herself up straighter.

"Only at night?" Jeff said, his voice incredulous. He sank into a tired-looking vinyl chair opposite her and grinned. "You mean it's safe during the daytime?"

"Well," she answered cheerfully, "I wouldn't say it was exactly safe. But you don't have to carry an Uzi."

Jeff's grin vanished as he remembered one of the reasons he'd tightened security at his own warehouse. "What kind of security do you have?"

Hannah blinked, surprised by the abrupt question. "We lock the place up at night, of course, and the windows are covered with bars."

"But the doors aren't locked during the daytime, are they? Anyone could walk in."

Hannah laughed. "Of course, anyone can walk in. That's the whole point. The local churches and synagogues that fund us insist a community center be open and available to the community it serves."

"I see." Jeff smiled wryly. "Sorry. I didn't mean to sound critical. It's just that we've had some problems at our warehouse in Oakland and I couldn't help but wonder what kind of safety precautions they have for the staff."

He suddenly felt fiercely protective of her. But he was wise enough to keep it from showing.

"We're about as security conscious as any business that operates in the inner city," Hannah answered with a negligent shrug.

"You do have a security parking lot, don't you?"

His question was so utterly serious, she laughed again. "You've got to be kidding. We don't have any parking lot. The staff parks on the street. Most of us don't have hubcaps anymore and all my friends think I'm crazy. But I think giving up a few car accessories is a small price to pay for having a job you love, don't you?"

"As long as that's the only price you pay," he said cryptically. "I take it your friends are shocked by your choice of employment?"

Jeff wondered if any of those "friends" she was referring to was a boyfriend who'd blown his stack when he'd seen where she worked. That would probably have been his own reaction.

"Definitely. When you say you work at a community center, this isn't the kind of place that springs to mind."

"That's true," he replied thoughtfully. He gazed around her office. The room was neat, freshly painted and clean. But the linoleum was dull and graying with age and the furniture looked as though it had come from a secondhand store. The only spots of color were a bright-red Say No To Drugs poster tacked on the wall and a small vase filled with pale yellow tea-roses on the corner of Hannah's desk.

He wondered who'd given her the roses. "I guess I pictured you in one of those modern stucco bungalows next to a big suburban church," he continued, dragging his gaze away from the flowers. "You know the kind of place I mean. One of those squeaky-clean all-American institutions designed to give wayward teenagers a wholesome environment and sweet little old ladies a place to play bingo on Wednesday afternoons."

Hannah burst out laughing. "What are you, psychic? You've just described our center in North County, including the bingo on Wednesday afternoons."

Her laughter—husky, seductive and decidedly sexy—was infectious. Jeff responded to the sweet sound and joined in. As the laughter faded, their gazes met and held. The moment turned intimate.

Hannah's smile slowly disappeared as the expression in Jeff's sky-blue eyes shifted and changed. He was staring at her mouth. She'd seen that look in a man's eyes before and usually, it had no effect on her. But now, a shiver coursed up her spine and her blood pumped madly through her veins, answering to the heat in his gaze.

"Well," she said firmly, "now that you're here, why don't you tell me why you've come."

Startled by her sudden change in mood, Jeff sat back in his chair and stared at her. She regarded him coolly, her expression friendly but impersonal.

Why was he here? He'd wondered the same thing himself. Part of the answer was obvious—he wanted to make sure she hadn't changed her mind about taking the test. But the other part, the part he didn't want to acknowledge, wasn't so clear-cut. He only knew he'd wanted to see her again—wanted to see her before she locked them both in a set of ironclad rules that dictated he and the rest of the Kenyons couldn't come near her.

"I came," he answered honestly, "to see if you'd changed your mind."

Her lips parted in surprise. "Of course not," she assured him, shaking her head. "I wouldn't do something like that. Honestly, I know how important this is. You wouldn't have gone to all the trouble and expense of hiring a detective to find me if your family wasn't desperate."

Jeff watched her impassively. Deep down, he'd known she wouldn't back out of the blood test. He'd only used that as an excuse to see her again.

"Why did you think I might?" Hannah asked curiously.

He smiled ruefully. "I was afraid that after you'd had time to think about it, about how disruptive to your life the whole thing might be, you'd decide not to bother."

"That would be pretty cold, wouldn't it?"

"Yes," he agreed. "But on one level, it would be understandable. You're intelligent enough to realize that if you are compatible with my sister, it's going to make an impact on your life. Change things for you—maybe even more than you'd like."

"All it will do," she countered bluntly, "is send me to San Francisco for a couple of weeks. And I assure you, that's no problem. I told you yesterday I can get all the time off that I need."

She was deliberately misunderstanding him and they both knew it. But Jeff decided to back off. For now. There'd be time enough later to bring up the subject of her meeting Kirsten and Irene.

"I guess I'm lucky that your employers are so understanding."

"Wouldn't *you* be?" Hannah asked with genuine interest. "I mean, if one of your employees needed time off for something like this, wouldn't you give it?"

"I would," he admitted. "But frankly, before Kirsten was diagnosed, I hadn't had any personal encounters with family emergencies." He shook his head. "This experience has really opened my eyes." He watched her carefully, his eyes somber. "Like I said, sometimes things change us in ways we never expected."

The underlying message beneath his words couldn't have been clearer if he'd written a memo and put it on her In tray, Hannah thought ruefully. Jeff was subtly hinting that now she knew about her birth family, she couldn't pretend they didn't exist.

He was dead wrong. Hannah swallowed nervously and said, "Well, I'm sure your employees appreciate your new attitude."

Jeff glanced at his watch. "Will you let me drive you to the clinic? That's the other reason I came down here. I thought you might like some company."

"That's not necessary," she replied hastily. "I have my own car."

"But I'd really like to," he persisted, his tone hopeful and eager. "You're doing us a big favor. Come on, let me play chauffeur. It's the least I can do."

She stared at him thoughtfully and then shrugged. Maybe she should let him drive her to the clinic. Maybe if she let him do a few little things for her, his gratitude wouldn't be so embarrassingly obvious.

"All right," she agreed. She stood and turned to pull her purse out of the top drawer of the filing cabinet.

Jeff liked the graceful way she moved. She was wearing a winter-white tailored shirtdress, and when she turned away from him, he couldn't help the way his gaze slid down her long, straight back, past the slim circle of her waist and on to the curves of her delightfully shaped backside.

Hannah tucked her purse under her arm and whirled back to her desk. He shifted in his chair as a slow, sexual heat sparked to life in his loins.

Completely oblivious to the effect she was having on him, Hannah smiled innocently and reached over to close the folder on her desk. Like a magnet, his gaze

was drawn to her chest. The dress she wore had a deep
V neck and as she bent over, the loose material gaped
open and gave him a clear view of her breasts. The
heat between his thighs hardened into hot desire.

Shocked by the way his body had reacted to her, he
leaped to his feet before he embarrassed himself.

It certainly isn't the Free Clinic, Hannah thought as
Jeff pulled open the heavy glass doors of the medical
building and ushered her inside. She smiled wryly as
she looked around the huge, luxurious lobby. The
room was filled with expensive furniture, expensive
plants and expensive people.

She glanced up at Jeff. He grinned knowingly.

"You've probably guessed this place doesn't do
charity work," he said, leading her toward the recep-
tion desk. "But Kirsten's doctors made all the arrangements. They have their own lab on the premises
and they've guaranteed to process your test immediately. We do have a time factor to consider."

Hannah wasn't sure why he was bothering to explain. Maybe after seeing where she worked he was
embarrassed about his wealth. She flicked him a quick
look from beneath her lashes. He was wearing the
same jacket he'd had on yesterday, jeans and a white
sport shirt. But the watch on his wrist was expensive
and the after-shave he wore didn't come from a dime
store.

Surreptitiously she edged closer to him and filled her
lungs with his clean, woodsy scent. On the drive over,
she'd been conscious of him in a way that she hadn't
been aware of a man in years.

She'd fought to keep from responding to him. But
there was one small part of her—the deeply buried

feminine part of her—that didn't give a damn about anything except reacting to the sensual attraction this man held for her.

And what was worse, she sensed he was equally attracted to her.

All of her senses went on red alert. The intensity of her feelings frightened her. He was dangerously, potently male, and everything about him affected her powerfully.

The sound of his husky voice speaking to the receptionist sent a shiver running down her spine. The sight of his long, tanned hands splayed on the top of the counter conjured up forbidden fantasies of dark hands on her pale flesh; and the heady scent of his warm body standing so close to hers sent her blood rushing through her veins.

For a moment, for one tiny instant in time, Hannah relaxed her guard and gave in to the sensual impulses flooding her body. She felt safe. After today, she'd never see him again. So why shouldn't she enjoy him for a few stolen moments? He'd never know.

"Oh, yes," chirped the receptionist, smiling brightly at Hannah. "We'll be ready for Miss Breckenridge in a moment."

Hannah started at the sound of the girl's voice. She smiled weakly and looked away. Her attention was caught by the door opening on the other side of the room. A middle-aged woman came out. She had a large bandage on the inside of her elbow.

Hannah's gaze was glued to the bandage. She grimaced, thinking of the needle.

"Would you like me to come in with you?" Jeff asked softly, seeing her expression.

She started to tell him no, but then quickly changed her mind. The truth was, she was a bit of a coward, and right now she didn't care if he knew it. "Yes," she replied quickly as a nurse popped her head out and called Hannah's name. "Yes, please."

A few moments later Hannah was holding out her arm and warily watching a white-coated lab technician with a syringe in his hand.

She closed her eyes and turned her head as the needle came toward the inside of her elbow.

Trying to distract her, Jeff reached over and cupped her chin. "Hey," he teased, "don't tell me you're scared of a little old needle."

"I am not," she protested feebly, trying not to look at her arm. She flinched as the needle entered a vein. Jeff let go of her chin and reached for her other hand.

He gripped her fingers tightly, his thumb moving in slow circles over her knuckles. "It'll be over in a minute," he murmured softly.

"I'm all right," Hannah said, incredibly distracted by his warm fingers. "I just hate watching them go in."

"So do I." He squeezed her hand lightly and Hannah felt electrical sparks shoot through her veins. A second later it was all done.

Every muscle in her body tightened as she pulled away and saw Jeff staring at the small vial the technician popped into a metal rack.

One of his eyebrows rose and his lips parted as he dragged in a deep, slow breath. She watched him gaze long and hard at the tube of blood, almost as though he were willing it to be a match with Kirsten's.

She didn't have to be clairvoyant to know what was going through his mind. This was his sister's last chance.

Neither of them said a word as they walked back to the car. Jeff opened the door on the passenger side and politely helped Hannah inside.

"How about some lunch?" Jeff asked as he slid behind the wheel. Keeping his gaze straight ahead, he shoved the key into the ignition and turned on the engine.

Hannah wondered if he was only being polite or if he really wanted company. She glanced at him and what she saw sent a wave of sympathy washing over her. He stared vacantly out the front window, his jaw rigid and his face a mask of tension.

She couldn't leave him. Not now. Hannah was no psychologist, but she knew he didn't need to be alone after the grim reminder of the blood test.

"I'd love some lunch," she replied lightly.

"Good." He turned and glanced at her. Then he smiled broadly. The tight lines of his jaw relaxed and the light came back into his eyes.

Hope is a powerful emotion, she thought briefly, turning to gaze out the window. Almost as powerful as gratitude.

"There's a few things I want to talk to you about," he continued casually. A bit too casually, Hannah thought uneasily.

"Like what?" she asked warily.

Jeff caught the thread of caution in her tone. "Like what kind of food do you want? Any preferences?"

"Anything's fine," she murmured, momentarily relieved. She kept her gaze straight ahead, struggling to marshal her emotions into some semblance of order. The implications of the blood test and what it could mean to her life were finally sinking in. She had to make her position perfectly clear to him. She had to make him understand that she would help, but she wouldn't become involved with either him or his family. It was too damned dangerous.

Maybe it would be best to go on the offensive before he made too many assumptions.

"Jeff, what do you want to talk to me about? If it's anything to do with my condition for helping, then forget it. I've told you. I can't have anything to do with your—" she hesitated "—stepmother or my sister."

His face tightened fractionally, but he didn't answer her. Jeff wasn't giving up. Whether Hannah realized it or not, she was already a part of their lives.

An awkward silence filled the car until she dutifully directed him into the parking lot of a local seafood restaurant.

The tension between them eased somewhat as Jeff ordered a Scotch and Hannah a glass of white wine. She didn't ordinarily drink at lunch, but today she decided her nerves needed it. She eyed him cautiously across the white linen tablecloth. He was deep in thought but he didn't look depressed or anxious.

Hannah cleared her throat. "What do you do at Kenyon International?" That was a safe enough question. Talking about his work would at least keep him off the subject of families.

"I'm the president."

Surprised, she blinked. "You're the president! You run the company? But you're so young."

"Don't let the fancy title fool you," he said with a boyish grin. "I'm still quite capable of driving a truck or operating a forklift if I have to."

Since he'd discarded his jacket when they sat down, her gaze was irresistibly drawn to his chest. Hannah could see the width of his shoulders, the strength in the smooth muscles beneath the sleeves of the short-sleeved sport shirt. Her attention moved down his arms and lingered on his hands. She could imagine those fingers gripping the steering wheel of a huge eighteen-wheeler, or shifting the gears of a forklift. But she could also remember how gentle they'd been when he'd cupped her chin to distract her from the needle. She swallowed and hastily snatched up her menu. "Yes," she replied faintly. "I can imagine."

"And what about you? How on earth did someone like you end up at a place like the Inner-City Community Center?" He deliberately kept his voice casual but he tensed as he waited for her answer. He needed Hannah to verify what he already suspected.

Hannah looked up from her menu and shrugged. "Why shouldn't someone like me work there? I saw the job advertised in the newspaper, applied for it and was hired. It's important work and I'm very good at it."

"Of course it's important work," he agreed quickly. "I'm not questioning that. As a matter of fact, I admire you for doing it. God knows, this old world needs people like you in it. But I will admit you make me curious. In this day and age of rampant over-achievers, it's rare to find a beautiful, intelligent woman doing a job that probably pays a pittance and doesn't provide more than the most basic of benefits."

Hannah drummed her fingers on the tablecloth, trying to decide whether or not he was criticizing her. But he didn't look disapproving; merely interested.

"Okay," she said with a shrug. "You're right. I could do better—at least financially. But I don't want to."

Jeff grinned. "Are you independently wealthy?"

"No," she answered with a laugh. "But I do believe some things are more important than money. And I know what I'm talking about, too. I've had good jobs in the past. But none of them were near as satisfying as what I'm doing now."

He was insatiably curious about her. "What did you do before?" he asked.

"When I graduated from college I worked for a large advertising agency in Los Angeles. It was very sleek, very chic and very west-side L.A. Before I knew it, I was in charge of administration. I made plenty of money, had a lovely apartment, drove a snazzy sports car and spent lots of weekends skiing at Lake Tahoe." Hannah paused and shook her head. "But it got old fast. I felt useless, like a parasite. Eventually I figured there had to be more to life than doing my bit to sell more deodorant or toothpaste." She broke off and fixed her gaze over his shoulder. "Then my father got sick and I moved down here to be close to him. I decided to stay. When the job at the community center came along, I jumped at it."

"Your father was a minister, wasn't he?" Jeff said, thinking of the photograph he'd seen in her apartment.

She nodded. "Yes. That's probably why I got dissatisfied so quickly at Seevers and Stone. After spending my whole life watching my parents working to help others, I felt a little guilty. But I'm satisfied now.'' She smiled brilliantly, her pride in her job obvious. "My job doesn't pay much and you're right about the benefits not being very good, but it's rewarding in every way that counts.''

A slow, lazy smile spread across Jeff's face. Hannah pursed her lips, puzzled at the unmistakable look of satisfaction in his gaze. She didn't understand. He'd been grilling her about her reasons for working at the community center and yet now he was looking at her as though she'd just announced she was being nominated for sainthood.

The waiter interrupted Hannah's speculations. She ordered a shrimp salad and decided not to worry about Jeff's motivations anymore. After today, she'd never see him again. Whatever happened with the test results, his part in this was over. So, trying to figure him out was a waste of time and energy. But the thought of never seeing him again brought a sharp stab of disappointment. Hastily Hannah brushed the uncomfortable feeling aside.

"That's enough about me,'' she said briskly. "How did you get to be president of Kenyon at such a young age?'' Talking about herself was making her nervous. She'd already revealed far more than she wanted him to know.

"Simple,'' he replied, picking up his Scotch. He took a sip and grinned at her over the rim. "Nepotism.''

"What?''

Jeff laughed. "My father started out with one used truck about twenty years ago. He worked hard and built the business up. By the time I got out of high school, he had lots of used trucks and a warehouse that looked worse than the community center. He'd also taken on a partner. But the partner split when the business hit some hard times. So instead of going off to college, I started loading freight and driving trucks. Between the two of us, we managed to get the company back on its feet. The rest, as they say, is history. And that's how I ended up president of Kenyon International at the tender age of thirty-four."

"Your father didn't mind you taking over the business?"

"No. Dad always liked being an operations man and I seemed to have a flair for running the business. He was more than happy to step down and let me take over. As long as I keep my nose out of the traffic department, we get along great."

"That doesn't sound like nepotism to me," she said dryly. Hannah reached for her wineglass, uncomfortably aware of a rising sense of admiration for this man. "It sounds like a lot of hard work. Not many young men would sacrifice their education to help their family save an ailing business."

"You make me sound very noble," Jeff said with a rueful smile. "I'm almost embarrassed to admit I did manage to go to college. Night classes. It took me a little longer, but eventually I got my degree. I majored in psychology."

Good Lord, Hannah thought, he was going to sprout a halo and wings next. Not only was he attractive, but he had character and personality, too. The thought filled her with dismay.

Why couldn't Jeff have been a boring, one-dimensional businessman obsessed with the fast track to success? It would be easy to forget him if that were the case. But he wasn't. He was a thinking, caring and sensitive human being who intrigued her more and more, every time he opened his mouth.

It would be too easy to like this man. Too easy to respond to the warmth and promise in those clear blue eyes of his. Too easy to give in to that insidious spark of attraction she could feel struggling to burst into flame.

But she wouldn't. It was much too dangerous—the way shooting off firecrackers was dangerous. For a brief moment, you were dazzled by a brilliant shower of sparkling beauty; but when the smoke cleared, all that loveliness and all that magic would have faded to nothing.

Chapter Four

"You look like you're about to fall out of your chair."

Jeff's teasing voice interrupted Hannah's introspection. She raised her gaze and smiled weakly.

"What's so unusual about me having been a psych major?" he asked.

"Uh, n-nothing," she stammered quickly. The arrival of the waiter with their lunch gave her a moment to recover. His college major hadn't particularly surprised her; it was her own reaction to discovering yet another fascinating aspect of his personality that was scaring the daylights out of her. "It's just...well, I would have thought you'd have studied business administration or finance."

Jeff shrugged. "I was interested in people. Everything I needed to know about business, I learned the hard way—by doing it." He grinned and took a bite of his swordfish. "But psychology is a fascinating subject, isn't it? And considering where you work, it gives us something in common, doesn't it?"

"That's true," she agreed politely, wishing he hadn't pointed out that particular fact to her. "But basically, I'm just an administrator." She picked up her fork and toyed with her salad. "Did you ever plan on going further? You know, getting a masters or a doctorate and becoming a psychologist?" The instant she asked the question, she silently cursed. What was she doing? Why did she keep asking him about himself? Damn, she didn't want to get to know him better, and she certainly didn't want to hear about how much they had in common.

He smiled and she could tell he was pleased by her interest. "No," he replied. "I just wanted my B.A. I've always known my future was at Kenyon."

"But if you genuinely liked the subject," she pointed out, unable to stop herself, "maybe you'd have been happier having a job where you could use it."

He shook his head. "No," he declared firmly. "I like what I do. Besides, I use the principles I learned in my psych classes all the time."

"Really?"

"Sure. Business is people. The bottom line is if you know what makes human beings tick, what really motivates them, you've got a good chance of running a successful operation."

"And you think you know what makes people tick?" Hannah promised herself she'd shut up in just a minute. But right now she was simply too intrigued by what he was saying to let it go.

"I think I know what motivates my staff," he replied. "And it isn't just getting a paycheck every two weeks."

She leaned toward him. "That's a very enlightened attitude," she said, hooked now, despite her promise to herself. "Do you apply the same principles when you're dealing with other, shall we say, less progressive members of the business community?"

Jeff gave her a puzzled frown and she hastily explained. "I mean, don't all those high-minded ideals put you at a disadvantage in the marketplace. From what little exposure to the transportation industry I've had, I'd have thought it was downright cutthroat?"

"Business is tough, all right," he agreed. "Especially the transportation business. But we do all right."

"There's no such thing as unethical practices or unfair competition in the trucking business?" She wasn't asking him about his company, she was asking him about himself.

His expression hardened. "Sure, there is," he said softly. "But I know how to handle that, too."

"Precisely how do you handle it?" Hannah sat back and waited for him to reveal yet another aspect of his character—a less than admirable trait that would give her something negative to cling to and use as a shield against this frighteningly powerful attraction. It wouldn't be anything horrible or ghastly, it would merely be a typical businessman's approach to handling the competition. And if she were lucky, after hearing about it she wouldn't like him as much.

He regarded her thoughtfully from across the table. Finally he answered, "If the competition gets a little too close to the edge or cuts one corner too many, then we play hardball." He smiled grimly. "We may have principles, but we don't roll over and play dead if the going gets rough. I take care of my people and I never bluff. And my competitors know it."

Jeff hadn't raised his voice, but a ripple of unease ran down Hannah's spine as she stared at him. He was saying he'd do what was necessary. Nothing more, nothing less. He'd simply use every resource at his disposal to ensure his company survived.

And there had been another message in his words. She had the distinct feeling he wasn't just telling her about how he ran his business, he was telling her about how he ran his life. Suddenly she wanted to get the conversation back to his employees. That was safer.

"Well," she said brightly, "Kenyon is certainly unusual. I've never heard of any other place that seemed more concerned with their employees' needs than with making a profit."

"Good Lord, woman, bite your tongue!" he exclaimed. "I didn't mean to give you that impression. Of course, we want to make a profit. That's the bottom line."

"Sorry," Hannah apologized. "But you did make it sound like Kenyon could be a perfect model for democracy in the workplace."

"It's more like an enlightened monarchy."

"And you're the king?"

"Best job to have, wouldn't you agree?" He grinned. "But at Kenyon, we try to balance things out a little. Every employee from the janitor on up is allowed some say in the decisions affecting their jobs. If there's a problem in any one department, the people responsible for doing the job are the ones we ask for answers."

''Your company must be a nice place to work,'' she remarked.

''We're not perfect, but we try,'' he said.

Hannah shrugged. His words impressed her. *He* impressed her, and that was the last thing she needed. She forced herself to remember why she'd accepted his invitation to lunch in the first place. She was only here to cheer him up, to keep his mind off that vial of blood and everything it represented. She gave Jeff a polite, impersonal smile. ''You seem to take care of everything at Kenyon.''

''Not everything,'' he said. ''We can provide food, shelter and warmth with our paychecks and a sense of status and security with our personnel policies. But there's a couple of basic issues we let the staff deal with on their own.''

''Like what?'' she said absently.

''The ones that really count.'' He smiled enigmatically. ''We do a lot for our employees, but we draw the line at the big things. You know—tenderness, love and affection. Enlightened management practises only go so far.''

He deliberately kept his voice casual. But this was too good an opening to miss. He felt a twinge of guilt at the way he was blatantly maneuvering her into more personal subjects, but he quickly suppressed the feeling. He wanted to get to know her, wanted to understand how her mind worked.

A knot of tension sprouted in Hannah's stomach. She didn't want to have a long heart-to-heart chat with Jeff Kenyon about emotional needs. That was really stepping too close to the fire. She picked up her wineglass and took a sip as she mentally groped for something to say.

"Does that mean Kenyon has a policy against dating in the workplace?" Hannah asked teasingly. "Isn't that a bit archaic?"

Oh, Lord! she thought, the instant the words were out of her mouth. Talk about saying something stupid. Where had that little gem come from?

Jeff shrugged. "I was talking about genuine emotional needs, not our staff's dating habits. Though I will admit, sex and romance are pretty important drives, too. But, to answer your question. No, we don't have a policy against office romances. It's none of our business what our employees do, as long as they do their jobs."

Hannah dropped her gaze. She crossed one arm defensively over her stomach and picked up her fork. Determinedly she attacked the food in front of her. She felt nervous and threatened. Every time she opened her mouth she seemed to walk right into a subject that either made her uncomfortable or made him more fascinating. She wished they could talk about something nice and dull and boring.

Jeff watched her from beneath his half-lowered eyelids. Though she was daintily eating her salad, her body language was fairly screaming a warning. And the message was perfectly clear: back off.

"How about you?" he said conversationally. "What did you major in?"

Startled, she lifted her head and blinked. Good God, she wondered, could the man read minds, as well? He'd found a boring topic, all right. "I majored in business."

He laughed and reached for his glass of Scotch. "Here I am, a psych major running a business, and you a business major working at a community center. Goes to show how surprising life can be at times.''

''Yes,'' she agreed uneasily. ''It's strange how life works out.''

She frowned when she saw how late it had gotten. ''We'd better hurry. I've got two meetings scheduled this afternoon and I want to make sure that grant proposal makes the evening mail.'' Hannah sighed. ''I want to get as much as possible done in case I have to leave for San Francisco.''

When she looked up, he was staring at her with an expression of such despair that it was painful.

''I'm sorry,'' she said quickly. ''I didn't mean that the way it sounded. I hope to God I do have to leave. I hope I am compatible with Kirsten.''

''Hey, don't look so worried. It's okay. I know what you meant.'' His face relaxed fractionally but the fear was still in his eyes.

It flashed through her mind that he was deliberately letting her see the true extent of his need and vulnerability. Jeff was the kind of man who could hide his feelings when he wanted to.

So why was he letting her see his pain? Did he already trust her—a complete stranger—that much? Hannah didn't want to think about that. She hastily looked down at her half-eaten food.

''I'm praying that you will have to leave,'' Jeff said softly. He reached across the table and put his hand on hers. ''I'm sorry if it puts a strain on your work.''

She stared at the large, tanned hand covering hers and tried to ignore what the warmth of his skin was doing to her pulse rate.

''Don't be sorry,'' she replied, forcing herself to meet his gaze. ''Compared to what your family is going through, problems with my workload are not important."

"They're your family, too, Hannah," Jeff said quietly.

She drew back and pulled her hand away. In as normal a voice as she could manage, she asked, "When will we get the test results?"

For a split second, Hannah thought she saw disappointment in his eyes. But then she figured she was mistaken. His voice was normal when he answered her.

"Usually it takes about a week. But the lab promised to rush it, and we might know as early as Friday." Jeff sighed inwardly and sat back in his chair. He'd known it wasn't going to be easy. He stared at her for a long moment. "If you are a match with Kirsten, can you be ready to leave by Monday?"

Hannah took a deep breath and smiled. "Yes."

Jeff drove the streets of San Diego with such ease that Hannah was surprised. When she asked him how he was so familiar with a town four hundred miles from his home, he told her he was in the area a lot on business. That knowledge unsettled her further.

Jeff pulled up to the curb in front of the center and started to open his door, but she was too quick for him.

"Please," Hannah said hurriedly, fumbling for the handle on her side of the car. "Don't get out. I can see myself in." She bid him a hasty goodbye and practically jumped out of the car.

He watched her walk gracefully into the center, his gaze drawn to the rhythmical sway of her hips. She was still wary of him.

Putting the car in gear, he frowned as he pulled out into the traffic. Why was she insisting on such a peculiar condition as the price of her help? She didn't seem bitter about having been given up for adoption. Or if she was, it certainly didn't show in her personality. And after seeing where she worked, he knew she wasn't cynical or hard-hearted. Then why did she insist the Kenyon family stay away from her?

"Mom." Hannah opened the door of her mother's house and stepped inside. She looked around the empty living room and frowned. "Mom, are you home?"

"In here, honey." Mary's muffled voice came from the back of the house. "I'll be out in a second."

Hannah waited in the living room, struggling to get a grip on herself. She'd spent the day on an emotional seesaw and the strain was beginning to tell on her. No matter how hard she'd tried to concentrate on her work, all she'd been able to think of was Kirsten Kenyon and the blood test.

Then she'd think of her mother.

She'd always prided herself on her ability to make decisions. That was one of her strengths as an administrator. But she still hadn't a clue about whether or not to mention the Kenyons to her mother. The thought of triggering another depression was unbearable; yet the idea of lying to Mary was even worse.

All the way up the San Diego Freeway she'd mentally debated the best course of action, and now she felt like a Ping-Pong ball. As she'd turned onto the Off ramp an old jumping-rope chant had popped in her head. "Yes-no-maybe-so-certainly. Yes-no-maybe-so-certainly. For the last three miles, the silly refrain had echoed continuously through her mind.

She still didn't have the faintest idea if she should mention the possibility of her going to San Francisco. Why take the risk of upsetting her mother when the test could still turn out to be negative?

Hannah turned and tossed her handbag onto a chair next to the door. Her eyebrows drew together when she saw her mother's coat neatly spread across the back. Mary's car keys and purse were sitting on top of it.

A door closed down the hallway and Hannah looked up to see her mother rushing toward her, her arms outstretched.

"Oh, Hannah, I'm so sorry. I'm just on my way out." Mary gave her a warm smile and a hug. "After working you so hard yesterday at that bake sale, I was sure you'd hide from me for the next three weeks."

Mary Breckenridge was a slender, petite, attractive woman blessed with the natural blond hair of her Nordic ancestors. She could still turn heads when she walked into a room. At least she could until recently, when her husband's death had seemed to age her almost overnight.

"Mom, you look fabulous!" Hannah exclaimed with a delighted smile. Mary was wearing her best red silk dress and two-inch patent-leather heels, and for the first time in months she'd put on makeup. "Are you going out?"

"You needn't sound so shocked," Mary replied with a laugh. "I do occasionally spend an evening somewhere other than in front of the television set. But it's nothing exciting. Just church work. Pastor McMahon and I are doing home communions at the convalescent hospital and then we're going to have a bite to eat.''

"You've got a date? With the pastor?"

"It's not a date," protested Mary. "It's church work. After all, I am an elder and I've got to do my part. Besides, we'll probably just stop at a coffee shop. But John needed someone to help with the communions.''

"Don't explain. I'm glad you're going. He's a nice man and you should start getting out more." Hannah beamed at her mother and almost laughed aloud when Mary blushed. She felt as though she'd been handed a reprieve. Only an idiot would say anything tonight.

Mary shrugged to cover her embarrassment and walked over to the mirror next to the door. Pulling a set of pearl earrings out of her pocket, she clipped one on and asked, "How come you came by? Not that I don't love seeing you, dear. Did you want to have dinner? You know, I can call John and ask—"

"Don't be ridiculous, Mom. You go on out and have a good time."

"But John won't mind."

"Mom," Hannah explained quickly, "I didn't stop by for dinner." She walked over and stood behind Mary. Their eyes met in the mirror and Hannah was struck again by how little resemblance there was between them. For a split second, she wondered if she looked like Irene Kenyon. Instantly she banished the disloyal speculation, but she wasn't fast enough to stop the inevitable stab of guilt that came with it.

As though she were afraid her thoughts were showing in her eyes, Hannah dropped her gaze. She busied herself smoothing her mother's collar and told herself to stop being absurd.

Of course she wondered if she looked like her birth mother. It was perfectly natural. Anybody would. Yet why did she feel as though she'd just committed treason? But she already knew the answer, and it brought no comfort. Her mother would be deeply hurt if she suspected that Hannah had spent half her life staring at auburn-haired strangers.

"Are you sure, dear?" Mary turned and watched her anxiously. "John wouldn't mind if you joined us. He's very interested in your work at the community center."

"No, Mom. Actually I just stopped by to see if you'd recovered from the bake sale. You must have been exhausted."

Mary laughed. "So were you. But believe it or not, I enjoyed all that activity. Mind you, I did have to soak my feet for an hour after I got home. But it was worth it. We made over seven hundred dollars for the deacon's fund."

"Seven hundred bucks! From selling a few cookies."

"We sold more than a few cookies, I'll have you know, young lady." Mary clipped on the other earring and moved toward the couch. "I baked for three solid days, and so did every other woman in the congregation."

There was a soft knock on the front door. "That's probably John." Mary rushed over and snatched her purse off the couch. She picked up her keys, grabbed her coat and then turned to smile at Hannah. "Are you sure you won't come with us?"

"Absolutely. I'm too tired tonight to even think of going out." Hannah picked up her jacket and slipped it on. She took Mary's arm and ushered her quickly to the door. "I'm going straight home to soak in a hot bath. Then I'm going to put my feet up, microwave a pizza and read a murder mystery. Go on, now, and have a great time. Stop worrying about me. I'll be just fine."

But later that night, Hannah found she couldn't concentrate on her paperback thriller. She kept thinking about Jeff Kenyon and wondering where he was and what he was doing.

By Friday afternoon, Hannah's nerves were stretched to the breaking point. Totally exasperated, she frowned at the disheveled young man lounging on a motorcycle and effectively blocking her from reaching the sidewalk. Hoping Jeff hadn't called with the test results while she was at lunch, she edged toward the curb.

"Kirby," she explained for the third time, "you know what the rules are. If you want a bed at the Children of God Homeless Shelter, you have to listen to a sermon."

"Jeez, what a drag." Kirby Dennison tugged his torn blue T-shirt down another inch over his bulging stomach and eyed Hannah speculatively. He reached up and shoved a lock of his curly brown hair back under the greasy yellow headband he wore. "What a dumb drag."

Hannah sighed inwardly. The Friday-afternoon battle was on. She knew she didn't have the stamina to go ten rounds with Kirby over where he could crash for the night. She was too preoccupied with worrying about the blood-test results and Kirsten to play games with a sulky boy who fancied himself a weekend biker. Kirby Dennison could take himself back to his parents' million-dollar beach house in La Jolla and leave her in peace.

Her real priority was getting into her office and seeing if Jeff had called.

Her nerves didn't need this. Turning abruptly, Hannah started for the door of the community center when Kirby grabbed her elbow.

"Hey," he yelped, sounding surprised by her sudden departure. "How about giving me a chit to get into the center in North County?" He smiled at her hopefully. "The grub's better and the water's hot."

How about going home to Mommy? Hannah thought irritably as she stared at the hand on her arm. He'd inked-in a fake tattoo of the phrase Brain-Dead over his wrist. She was almost inclined to agree with him.

"That's impossible," Hannah answered, trying to shake off his grip. She wasn't alarmed. Kirby was harmless. "You've been banned from North County because of your mouth—"

"Let the lady go."

The hard voice made Kirby automatically lighten his grip. Hannah whirled around and found herself staring into Jeff's dangerously narrowed eyes.

"What are you doing here?"

Jeff didn't look at Hannah. He kept his gaze on the big hulk who still had ahold of her arm.

Kirby's eyes widened in alarm as Jeff took a step forward. He dropped Hannah's arm and backed toward his bike.

"Hey, man, I know the lady. I was just talking to her." He shifted awkwardly as he scrambled onto the motorcycle and started the engine. Kirby kept his eye on Jeff as he backed out of the parking space. But as he roared away he recovered enough to lift his hand and make an obscene gesture at Jeff.

Hannah stifled a giggle.

"Nice guy." Jeff glared at the disappearing motorcycle and then turned his attention to Hannah. "Is he typical of your clientele?" He didn't bother to hide the contempt in his voice.

Hannah's amusement died but Jeff didn't notice. He was too busy trying to control the rage pouring through his system. When he'd seen that jerk grab her arm, he'd seen red. He shook his head. Good God! Didn't the woman have any better sense than to mouth off to a biker twice her size in the middle of the street? He threw a scathing glance at the crowd sitting on the steps of the center. It was a sure bet none of them would have done a damned thing if the guy had turned violent.

Hannah's pulse quickened. She wasn't supposed to have to see him again. This was all wrong. Jeff was supposed to call her with the results, she remembered angrily. And why the hell was he interfering? For God's sake, she'd worked in this area for two years!

"Actually," she replied acidly, "Kirby's one of our better-behaved clients."

"Really?" Jeff's face hardened as he caught the sarcasm in her voice. "Then maybe you should get a new job. Unless you enjoy being manhandled on a public street."

"I wasn't being 'manhandled,'" she flared. "I knew exactly what I was doing." She paused and took a deep breath. Standing on the street and arguing with the man was stupid. He'd obviously come to see her.

"Now," she said in a voice cold enough to freeze water, "would you mind telling me what you're doing here?"

"That's pretty obvious," he muttered, glaring at the street corner where Kirby had disappeared. "I came to see you." The adrenaline was still pumping hard through his veins. "Do you have to put up with a lot of scenes like that?"

"I was handling it," Hannah snapped. "And you were supposed to call me." She turned and walked toward the door. She heard his footsteps as he trailed behind her. "And I didn't really appreciate your interference."

"Interference!" he exploded. "I was trying to help. It looked like that big ape was getting ready to attack you."

"Well, you weren't helping," she declared, pushing open the door. "I'm used to these people and I know how to cope with them."

He'd caught her off guard, hadn't given her time to prepare herself for seeing him. She was angry he'd shown up unannounced. They had an agreement, damn it, and he was violating it.

Hannah decided she'd better let this man know where the limits were. If she gave him an inch, he'd take a mile. She stalked across the noisy, crowded community center and headed for her office.

Jeff followed her. He paused inside the doorway and forced himself to calm down. He didn't want her upset, and he felt like a fool for letting his temper get the better of him. He had interfered, and he could understand her being angry. But, hell, it had looked as though the guy had been getting ready to jump her.

Hannah tossed her purse onto her desk and turned to face him. ''All right. What do you want?''

Jeff took a deep breath. ''The tests are back.'' He broke into a huge grin. ''You're compatible.''

Chapter Five

Jeff watched her carefully. Her eyes widened and her face paled. She swayed and he stepped toward her, thinking she might faint. "Are you all right?"

"Oh, yes," she replied in a husky whisper. Holding up her hand to reassure him, she sagged against the edge of her desk. Tears of joy filled her eyes and she bowed her head and said a quick, silent prayer of thanks.

"Hannah?" Jeff's voice was concerned.

Her head snapped up and she gave him a watery smile. "I'm all right," she told him. "I'm just so happy. I feel like singing the 'Hallelujah Chorus.'"

He broke into a huge grin. "Me, too. The whole family is on cloud nine over the news. For the first time in months, there's hope. Kirsten's got a chance now."

A rush of elation surged through Hannah. Her knees shook and her head spun. Now that there was a ray of hope—a real honest-to-God chance her half sister might make it—she could finally acknowledge how worried she'd been.

She'd been living in a state of siege since Jeff had burst into her life. His request had shaken her to the core. Her emotions had been under constant fire, battered by conflicting loyalties and repressed fears. The knowledge that her half sister—a sister she hadn't even known existed—might be dying had literally terrified her.

Hannah focused her gaze straight ahead and gave in to a blessed feeling of relief. She'd been worrying about Kirsten Kenyon for days. Worrying and hoping and praying.

Jeff threw his head back and laughed. "It's almost a miracle, Hannah. A miracle." Impulsively he picked her up and whirled around in a circle. She was surprised, but only for a second. Then she started laughing, too.

Holding her felt good, he thought. But as his arms tightened around her waist and he lifted her higher in the air, he quickly realized it wasn't just good; it was wonderful.

Hannah was still laughing, her arms were locked around his neck and her head was thrown back exposing the long, smooth lines of her throat. Picking her up had been a spontaneous gesture of affection on his part. But as his body tightened and every nerve ending tingled with sensual awareness, Jeff realized how attracted he was to her. He'd wanted her from the moment he saw her.

The urge to crush her to him, to kiss that lovely neck and bury his face in the softness of her hair was shockingly real.

He caught himself and came to a halt.

"I can't believe it." Hannah shook her head and swiped at an escaping tear. She was too happy to be embarrassed, too happy even to realize that Jeff hadn't let her go and was, in fact, still holding her high in the air. The only thing she could think of was Kirsten.

"I've been so worried," she said. "And now there's a chance. A real chance."

She looked down at him, her eyes shining. Their gazes met and held. An unspoken message arced between them as Jeff reluctantly eased her to the floor. Her feet had barely touched the linoleum before he gently brushed his mouth against hers.

The kiss was sweet and gentle. Hannah forgot her reservations, her vow to stay away from this man. For five days, she'd been wrapped in a cocoon of silent dread. She'd been alone, isolated and terribly afraid for her sister. Now it was as though a heavy burden had been lifted from her shoulders, and all she wanted was to share this moment with him.

But Jeff suddenly needed more. His desire had been locked inside him like caged heat, and the barriers were starting to come down. He pulled her closer and increased the pressure on her mouth. Surprised, Hannah gasped. His tongue slipped between her parted lips.

Beneath the anxiety and hope and the never-ending pain of worrying about his sister, Jeff's life-force pulsed with a will of its own. It drowned his common sense and overcame all his qualms. This woman was very special—he'd known that from the first—and now she was handing them a possible miracle. He let his mind go blank and his instincts took control.

Slowly, tenderly, his tongue stroked deeply into Hannah's mouth. He tensed in anticipation, and a heavy throbbing started in his loins.

At the first taste of his tongue, her pulses leaped and her blood sang. Pleasure flooded through her in a hot, rushing wave. She'd never known desire could come this quickly, this powerfully, and she was helpless against it.

He ran his hand down her spine, memorizing the curves and angles of her back while his other hand buried itself in the softness of her hair.

Neither of them heard the door open.

"Oops... Excuse me, Hannah." Jeremiah Charter's amused voice penetrated through her misty haze. Hannah jerked back and spun around. Her hand flew to her mouth as she stared into the staff psychiatrist's twinkling green eyes.

Jeremiah grinned. Hannah wished for an earthquake.

"So sorry," Jeremiah said smoothly. "I knocked but apparently you didn't hear me." He held out a set of manila folders. "Here are the files you were asking for this morning."

Swallowing her embarrassment, Hannah forced a polite smile. "Thanks. I appreciate your getting to it so quickly." She walked to the door and reached for the folders. Behind her, Jeff cleared his throat.

Remembering her manners, she introduced the two men. They shook hands and Jeremiah threw one last, knowing glance at Hannah before leaving the office.

"I'm sorry," Jeff said quietly as the door closed. "I didn't mean to embarrass you at work."

"You didn't embarrass me," Hannah lied. Aware of Jeff's eyes on her, she sighed and moved behind her desk. Oh, God! she thought miserably. This is so awkward. Her brain worked frantically to come up with a reason for what had just happened between them. She had to say something; letting him come to his own conclusions would be incredibly stupid.

"We've both been under a strain," she began hesitantly. "It was a relief to be able to release it by—" She broke off, searching for the right words.

"By my kissing you?" He finished for her. "I suppose that's one way of looking at it."

Like hell, he thought. What happened when they'd kissed was a lot more than just a release of tension. He knew it. But she looked wary again, and he didn't want to scare her off.

Deftly he changed the subject. "Can you be in San Francisco by Monday?"

"Yes." Hannah smiled in relief. "I've warned the board of directors I might be gone on a medical emergency. So I just have to inform them that it's now a fact."

Jeff frowned as he realized she'd used the term "medical emergency," not "family emergency." That wasn't a good sign. He'd hoped by now Hannah had started thinking of Kirsten as family.

"Great," he replied, shoving the issue of Hannah's word choices to the back of his mind. He reached into the pocket of his black corduroy jacket and pulled out an airline ticket. Handing it to her he said, "Here's a first-class ticket for the noon flight on Sunday. I thought you might need a day to get packed and take care of any last-minute details. I'll meet you at the airport and take you to a hotel near the hospital. Naturally, we'll pay all your expenses.''

Hannah gazed at the ticket for a moment but made no move to take it.

"Is there something wrong?" He dropped the ticket onto the desk and stared at her, his expression puzzled.

"Jeff—" she swallowed and felt a blush creep up her cheeks "—this is awkward, but there isn't any diplomatic way to say this." Hannah took a deep breath. "I can't accept that ticket. I've decided to pay my own expenses. It's very kind of your family to offer, but there's no need—"

"Now just hold on," he interrupted. "What's going on here? What are you talking about? Of course you'll take the ticket and let us pay your expenses. My God, we can afford it. You're doing us a favor—"

"Please." Hannah wasn't above interrupting, either. "I can't take it from you. After all, Kirsten's my half sister. I can't let your family pay my expenses. I'm not as rich as you are but that doesn't mean I can't afford to help my own sister."

She looked up at him stubbornly. Hannah was desperate to keep from owing the Kenyons anything. She didn't need any more guilt. Her condition for being a donor had haunted her all week.

Jeff was so surprised, it took him a few seconds to react. He leaned down and flattened his hands against the top of the desk. "I wasn't implying you couldn't afford to pay your own way," he said. "But don't you think you're being a little absurd? Less than a week ago, you'd never even heard of us and now you want me to sit back and let you shell out hundreds of dollars in hotel bills and airplane fares? We came to you asking for help. Remember?''

"That doesn't make any difference," she argued. "I know about Kirsten now. Just because I can't meet her or see her doesn't mean I don't care." Hannah shook her head. "No, I won't take any money for helping my own sister."

Their gazes locked in a battle of wills. They stared at each other for several seconds, both of them determined to win.

Then Jeff nodded abruptly, picked the ticket off her desk and slipped it inside his coat.

Hannah dropped her gaze and stared at the papers on the desk. She knew he meant well, knew he was only trying to do the right thing. But this was important to her. She wanted to give as much as she could to Kirsten—to the sister she would never get to know.

"I didn't say you didn't care about Kirsten," he said softly. "I just wanted to make this as easy on you as possible."

"I appreciate that," she replied with an uneasy smile. "But I want to do this."

"All right, we'll do it your way." Jeff sat down across from her. "Will you at least let me take care of your hotel reservations?"

"That won't be necessary. Just give me the details about the hospital and where I'm supposed to be. I'd prefer to make my own arrangements."

"Hannah, I wish you'd let us do something." Jeff tried to quell a rising sense of alarm. Surely she wasn't putting her condition into effect yet? He couldn't let her make her own reservations. She might not tell him where she was staying.

"My secretary's an expert in hotel reservations," he said, trying to keep his voice light. "The woman's incredible. She knows every deal in town. Come on, it's the least I can do. We'd like to show our gratitude in some way."

Gratitude.

Hannah felt as though she'd been slapped in the face. She stiffened. Of course they were grateful. Who wouldn't be?

But she was glad he'd reminded her—reminded her that no matter how his kisses could make her head spin, no matter how good it felt to be in his arms, she'd be a fool to read anything into it. Jeff Kenyon felt one thing and one thing only—gratitude.

With difficulty she kept a polite smile plastered on her face. "There's no need to do that," she said briskly, pulling a notepad out of her top drawer. "Just give me the pertinent details and I'll take care of the rest."

The view from Mary Breckenridge's backyard was impressive. Set on the crest of a hill, the Pacific Ocean in the distance, it afforded a sight that usually made Hannah feel serene. But today as she stared at the gray, overcast sky and sea, she felt anything but calm.

She'd hoped the euphoria of learning she was compatible with Kirsten could make this easier. But it didn't.

Behind her, she could hear her mother humming softly as she dug up a flower bed. Hannah glanced up at the slate-colored clouds and cleared her throat. "Mom?"

"Yes, dear?"

Mary's cheerful voice made her wince inside. Her courage deserted her. "Do you think it's going to rain?"

"I certainly hope so," Mary replied crisply. "We need the water. These dry winters have been terrible. If we don't get some decent rain this year, we're going to be on water rationing this summer."

"Mom..." Hannah hesitated. She'd run out of time. No more stalling. Tomorrow at noon she was getting on a plane for San Francisco. "I need to talk to you."

Disturbed by her daughter's somber voice, Mary paused and stared apprehensively at Hannah. "What is it, dear? You sound so serious."

Hannah sat down. The earth was cold and damp, but she was too intent on getting this over with to care about grass stains on her old jeans. "Mom, it *is* serious."

Mary tossed down the trowel and gave Hannah her full attention. Her blue eyes wide and puzzled, she wore a look of alarm on her face. "You're not ill or anything, are you?"

"No," Hannah said quickly. "I'm fine. There's nothing wrong with me. But there is something wrong with someone else, and I'm afraid I'm the only one who can do anything about it."

Some of the alarm faded from Mary's face but she remained silent.

Hannah took a breath and plunged ahead. "Last Sunday a man named Jeff Kenyon came to see me. He asked me for a favor. A big one. The upshot of his visit is that I have to go to San Francisco for a couple of weeks."

Mary frowned. "What kind of a favor did this man want? Is it something to do with the center? Did he offer you a job? Is that why you're going to San Francisco?"

"No," Hannah answered. "No, nothing like that. Jeff has a sister and she's got leukemia. Her only chance is a bone-marrow transplant. Jeff asked me to test for... donor compatibility."

Mary went perfectly still. The color drained out of her face. "Go on."

"I took the test on Monday." Hannah's stomach contracted as she watched her mother's expression. "Yesterday I found out I'm a match. I'll be leaving tomorrow."

Mary's face seemed to age ten years in the space of a few seconds. "Mom," Hannah whispered desperately, "I have to do this. She's only seventeen. And she's going to die if I don't help."

Mary closed her eyes and dropped her gaze to the half-dug flower bed. She inhaled sharply as a slow shiver racked her slender frame.

"Oh, Mother," Hannah said helplessly.

Mary's lower lip trembled for a moment, then she seemed to get ahold of herself. She drew herself up straighter and turned, looking directly into Hannah's eyes. "Why did this man come to you?" she asked. "What made him think *you* might be compatible?"

The question was rhetorical and they both knew it. Mary had spent twenty-five years as a minister's wife. She'd spent hundreds of hours visiting the sick with her husband. The mechanics of donors and cancer and devastating illnesses were no secret to her. She knew the answer. But, as Hannah had, she needed to hear it spelled out.

"She's my half sister."

"I see." Mary rose stiffly and brushed the dirt off her coveralls. Turning, she stared off into the distance at the ocean. Hannah watched her anxiously.

After a few moments, Mary turned to face her daughter. She wore a strained smile. "Forgive me, Hannah," she said gently. "I shouldn't have reacted the way I did. Of course, you have to go." She broke off and blinked rapidly. Hannah knew she was struggling to hold back tears. "This is quite a shock," she continued in a ragged voice. "I'll admit that. But if a young girl's life is at stake, my feelings aren't important."

"Oh, Mom!" Hannah leaped to her feet and put her arm around Mary's shoulders. "It was a shock to me, too. And your feelings *are* important. I wouldn't do anything to hurt you."

"I know that," Mary said with a watery smile. "You've always been a good daughter, but this isn't the time to be concerned about me."

Hannah felt wretched. She could see the agony in her mother's eyes. "You've got to believe me. Except for acting as a marrow donor, I'm not going to have anything to do with the Kenyons. The fact that Kirsten's my half sister is nothing more than a biological accident."

In the back of her mind, Hannah realized Mary wasn't asking the obvious questions.

Slowly Mary shook her head. "I can't ask that of you. You have a right to get to know your own sister."

Hannah's heart tightened painfully and a lump rose in her throat. Her mother would tell her to go, to do whatever she could to help save a human life. But every minute she was gone, Mary would be reliving what had happened with her other child—with the daughter she'd lost forever.

"Mama," Hannah went on intently. "I've got a family. I've got you—I don't need anyone else. I'm going to go to San Francisco to donate bone marrow. I'm not searching for my identity or looking for my roots. Please don't worry. You're my mother, my family. Nothing is ever going to change that."

"Oh, Hannah," Mary said wistfully, "you don't have to convince me of your devotion. I know you love me and I know I'll always be your mother. But you don't know what the future holds. You don't know how you're going to feel once you get to San Francisco. I know you're trying to make me feel better. But there's no need." She paused and took a deep breath. "The only thing that matters is your helping to give that girl another chance at life." Her expression suddenly clouded with concern. "There's no danger to you, is there?"

"No," Hannah said reassuringly. "Jeff's insisting I have a complete physical to make sure my body can handle it. For a healthy person, the procedure's perfectly safe."

Mary drove her to the airport the next day. Both women kept up a stream of idle chatter, trying to pretend everything was fine. But every time Hannah looked at Mary, she could see the worry and anxiety lurking in her mother's eyes.

She was suddenly glad Mary hadn't asked any more questions. At least she hadn't had to lie about her birth mother being in the picture. Hannah shivered and pulled her jacket tighter. Mary couldn't have handled that.

Her mother's fear of losing her daughter was too deeply ingrained to be smoothed over with a few words of reassurance. And it didn't matter that Mary's feeling was irrational—the things that frightened most people were often irrational.

It was raining when she landed at the San Francisco airport. Within an hour she was checking into the motel that Jeremiah Charter had recommended. The place was part of a national chain. It was neat, clean and conveniently located near the hospital where Hannah would be spending a good part of the next couple of weeks.

"I have a reservation," she said to the desk clerk. "My name is Breckenridge, Hannah Breckenridge."

"Oh, yes, here it is. We've been expecting you, Miss Breckenridge." He shoved a white card toward her and turned to pull a key off a rack behind him. "You were lucky we had a cancellation," he continued chattily. "The whole town is full. There's a record number of conventions this year. I'm sorry we're only able to accommodate you for two nights."

Distracted, Hannah heard his words but they didn't sink in. She kept seeing her mother's face and remembering Jeff's kiss. The combination had her nerves so on edge she had to concentrate to fill out the registration card.

"That'll be fine," she mumbled absently, trying to recall her home address. She completed the card and handed it back to the clerk. He was still chattering. Not having heard a word he'd said, Hannah smiled politely.

"Your room is up the stairs and to the right," he continued, handing her the room key. "Let us know if you need anything."

Gratefully Hannah took her key and escaped to the sanctuary of her room. As she unpacked, she told herself that at least she wouldn't have to see Jeff Kenyon anymore. The man was completely off-limits for her. Getting involved with him would only mean trouble. She knew that by the way her heartbeat skipped and her pulse rate soared every time she laid eyes on him. And the way he'd kissed her... Dear God, she'd never responded like that to a kiss!

Who knows what would have happened if Jeremiah hadn't interrupted? It had been so embarrassing; she'd never behaved like that in her life. The kind of physical attraction she'd felt was almost scary. Dangerous.

But she'd be on her guard now. She was attracted to Jeff and she was honest enough to admit it. But she wasn't fool enough to give in to it. Not when there were so many reasons to stay away from him.

She could still see the expression of gratitude on his face—a look she'd seen every time Kirsten's name was mentioned. That alone was reason enough to stay away from the man. And her mother! Mary's face flashed before her eyes and she bit her lip. No. She couldn't put her mother through any more.

Hannah's appointment with the doctor in charge of Kirsten's case wasn't until late Monday afternoon. Unable to stand staring at the walls of her motel room, she spent most of the day riding the cable cars and walking in Golden Gate Park.

Jeff was waiting for her when she arrived at the doctor's office. Hannah didn't see him at first. He'd been sitting behind a huge potted plant, reading a magazine. It was only as he rose to his feet that she realized he was there.

He smiled pleasantly. "Hello, Hannah. I'm glad you made it," he said politely. "Did you have a nice flight up?"

"H-hello," she stammered. "The flight was fine. I know I keep asking you this, but what are you doing here?"

"Waiting for you." For a brief moment, he almost felt as though he'd been waiting for her all his life. But he quickly squelched that fanciful thought.

Hannah frowned. Before she could remind him that his presence violated their agreement, he seized the offensive.

"Look," he said reasonably, "I'm not related to you, so relax. This involves my sister. I have a right to be here when you talk to the doctor. There are a few questions I need to ask."

"What questions?" she asked suspiciously. "What do you need to know? I thought everything was all set."

"It is. But there's one or two details I want to get straight."

Hannah released her tight hold on the doorknob and walked across the waiting room to the couch opposite Jeff. There was another door with Dr. Trevisi's name on it directly behind her, but Hannah ignored it. She wanted to get rid of Jeff before she saw the doctor.

"Like what?" she asked warily. "I can't see why you need to be here. The doctor and I are just going to go over the details of my medical tests and answer a few of each other's questions."

Jeff crossed his arms. "That's exactly why I'm here. I want to make sure they do everything possible to protect your health."

She sighed in exasperation. "I'm not the one at risk here."

"Believe me," he said with deep feeling, "I know that. But you might have some questions about Kirsten the doctor can't answer. I want to be in there—" he gestured with his hand toward the inner office "—in case something comes up. I'm not trying to snoop into your personal medical history. The whole point of this meeting is to acquaint you with the technical aspects of Kirsten's illness and the transplant procedure. Dr. Trevisi's the cancer specialist, but he isn't the one who diagnosed Kirsten. He may not be able to tell you everything."

Hannah hesitated. She wasn't sure if she believed him, but there was a chance he was right. Maybe she would have some questions about Kirsten. Sighing, she decided it was far better to talk to Jeff in front of the doctor than alone.

There was a soft click of a door being opened. Hannah turned and saw a tall, balding, middle-aged man in a white coat standing in the doorway.

"Good morning, Jeff." He smiled warmly at Hannah. "And this is our donor, I presume. Please—" he stood back and motioned them into his office "—come in and let's get started."

"Sit down." Dr. Trevisi gestured at two chairs in front of his desk. "I'm sure you must have a lot of questions," he said, looking at Hannah. "So, why don't we take care of that first."

Hannah was slightly flustered, but she quickly recovered. "First of all, I want to know how dangerous the procedure is."

"For you, there's very little danger."

"Not for me," she corrected hastily. "For Kirsten."

The doctor frowned and glanced uneasily at Jeff. Jeff shrugged.

"During the actual procedure itself," the doctor began cautiously, "there's very little danger. However, Kirsten faces substantial risks, including rejection of the donated marrow after the transplant." At Hannah's stricken expression, the doctor raised his hand. "However, if she doesn't have a bone-marrow transplant, she's got virtually no chance at all."

"You mean this isn't a guaranteed cure?" Hannah heard Jeff take a deep breath.

The doctor smiled sadly and shook his head. "There are no guarantees. But frankly, I wasn't overly optimistic we'd even find a donor." He grinned at Jeff. "But Jeff wouldn't give up. Even when I explained how remote the odds were that you'd be a match, he still insisted on locating you."

"Why would it be unusual that I'm a match?" Hannah asked curiously. "Kirsten's my half sister."

"Generally a match is found only between full siblings or from a parent. For a half sister to match so closely is very, very rare."

Nervously she cleared her throat. "But if the transplant takes, will Kirsten have a good chance for a complete recovery?"

"Yes. In many cases, there is what a layman would call a complete cure," Dr. Trevisi said cautiously. "Bone-marrow transplants are now considered a standard treatment in cases like Kirsten's, if a suitable donor is found. However, it's not all smooth sailing even if the new marrow is accepted into Kirsten's body. There are many things that can go wrong.''

''What kinds of things?''

''Infection is one of our biggest concerns,'' he explained. ''The body's major defense against infection, the white blood cells, can run very low after the procedure. But we do have ways to fight this—we keep the patient in isolation until the count is high enough to fight off any contagious bacteria or viruses.''

''You mean Kirsten has to stay in a plastic bubble or a sterile room after the operation?'' Hannah was horrified. Kirsten was just a teenager.

''Not just after the operation.'' Dr. Trevisi leaned back in his chair and regarded Hannah thoughtfully. ''She's in isolation now. In order for her to receive your bone marrow, she has to have a series of radiation treatments. Unfortunately those treatments also leave a patient vulnerable to infection.'' He smiled suddenly. ''But don't look so worried. Kirsten's a fighter. And believe me, that counts for a lot.''

Hannah swallowed. Her voice when she spoke was barely a whisper. ''Is she in a lot of pain?''

Jeff reached over and gently covered her hand. She turned and stared at him, seeing him through new and sympathetic eyes. How could he endure it? How could anyone endure knowing someone they loved was going through this?

''Hannah,'' Jeff said softly, ''they're doing everything they can to make her comfortable. Don't worry. Like the doctor said, she's one tough little fighter. She'll make it.''

Chapter Six

Jeff took Hannah's arm and guided her out of the doctor's office. Blindly she followed him toward the elevators at the end of the corridor.

She shook her head. "My God," she muttered softly, almost unaware she was speaking aloud. "That was a depressing surprise. I thought the transplant was a sure thing, a guaranteed success."

Jeff laughed harshly. "Like the doctor said, there are no guarantees."

Hannah felt like crying. She'd wrongly assumed that if she were compatible with her half sister, they were home free. But Dr. Trevisi had quickly dispelled that notion. Yet she wasn't about to give up, either.

"But Kirsten's a fighter," Hannah said doggedly, refusing to give in to depression. "Even the doctor said that counted for a lot."

Jeff's hand tightened on her arm as he steered her around an orderly pushing a gurney. They stopped in front of the elevator. "Yeah, Kirsten's a fighter, all right," he answered in a flat voice. "She's had to be."

He punched the call button. "I'm going up to her room. I want to say good-night and let her know you arrived safely."

Deliberately Hannah forced herself to shake off the vague sense of anxiety she'd been fighting since walking out of the doctor's office. She glanced at Jeff and her chest tightened in compassion.

On the surface he looked perfectly composed; his expression was carefully blank. But his eyes told a different story. Bleak and hopeless, they were filled with despair. Shaken, she stared at him for a long moment, realizing what he must go through every time he had to confront the facts about his sister's illness.

And it had been almost a miracle that she was even a match. My God, she thought, staring at the hard set of his jaw, Jeff's probably thinking two miracles in a row would be pushing our luck.

But I am a match! That must be a good sign. No, she amended quickly, it was more than a sign; it was a reason to hope and to believe in miracles.

Jeff glared at the elevator doors. He released Hannah's arm and savagely jabbed the call button again.

She hadn't been aware of him holding her elbow, but the minute the contact was broken she felt the loss. Yet, even without touching him, she sensed the depth of his frustration and pain. She didn't question this sudden ability to know what he was feeling—this strange empathy that had somehow sprung to life between them.

Later, it would no doubt bother her. But right now she was too concerned about Jeff to worry about anything else. This was the first time she'd seen him be anything but strong and optimistic. And it scared her.

Deciding to do something—anything to keep him from sinking further into despair—she smiled brightly and asked, "Do you want me to wait for you in the lobby?"

Jeff's head snapped up in surprise. Her smile widened. Startled, he hesitated a moment. "All right," he mumbled. "Sure, that's fine. I'll give you a ride back to your motel."

Hannah wasn't put off by his less-than-enthusiastic reaction. She knew he was probably wondering what was going on. She hadn't been overly gracious to him in the doctor's office. But she wasn't about to let him go off alone tonight and brood, either. That wouldn't do Kirsten or him any good.

She kept her smile firmly in place as the elevator arrived and Jeff stepped inside. His surprise was plain but he did nod slowly just as the door slid shut.

Jeff pondered Hannah's invitation as he made his way to the isolation wing of the oncology unit. But as he approached Kirsten's room, he pushed it to the back of his mind.

He couldn't let Kirsten see him this down. The kid was far too astute at sensing his moods, and it was vitally important she keep her spirits up. Jeff stopped outside the door to her room, took a deep, steadying breath and forced a smile to his lips.

Peering through the glass partition, he saw Kirsten sitting propped up in the bed, a book was open on her lap, and she was sipping something from a paper cup.

His spirits rose as he realized she wasn't hooked up to an IV. The smile on his face became genuine.

In the past two years, the whole family had learned a new meaning to the word *victory*. Even the smallest improvement became a cause for celebration. They'd learned to take their triumphs where they could and turn each tiny conquest into a treasured moment of jubilation.

On her head, Kirsten was wearing a pink cotton turban the same color as her bathrobe. The radiation treatments had made her hair fall out. Her face was pale and her body so thin and frail that she looked as though a puff of wind could blow her away.

Jeff tapped lightly against the glass and picked up the phone on his side of the partition. Kirsten lifted her chin and when she saw him, broke into a huge grin.

He couldn't go inside her room. Her environment had to be completely sterile. The whole family frequently scrubbed up and donned regulation hospital gowns and masks to go in to see her, but for short visits, they used a two-way telephone system to talk to each other.

Kirsten put the cup down and picked up the phone. "Hi, Jeff. You'll never believe what I talked them into making for me."

"What?" He asked suspiciously, watching her lift the cup in a mock salute toward him.

"A Suicide," she said, her hazel eyes sparkling.

"A what?"

"Oh, come on, Jeff. It hasn't been that many years since you played Little League." Kirsten giggled. "You can't have forgotten. Dad told me he used to let you drink one after you hit a home run."

"Oh, no." Jeff laughed and made a face at her. "Don't tell me they're letting you drink that concoction. What was it, now? Oh, yeah, I remember. It's a combination of cola, root beer, lemon-lime and orange soda." He shook his head. "And you're drinking that stuff? Voluntarily!"

"It tastes great," Kirsten announced, licking her lips. "Besides, it took me hours to talk Nurse Triggs into it. You remember her, don't you, big brother? She's the foxy blonde who's got the hots for you. I think that's why she made me the Suicide."

He laughed again. "You sound like you're feeling pretty chipper today."

"I'm fine." Kirsten's smile faded. "Is she here, yet?"

They'd told Kirsten about Hannah after the test results. Irene had been nervous about it. Admitting to having had an illegitimate child when she was the same age as Kirsten wasn't a mother's idea of fun. But Kirsten had been surprisingly mature about the whole thing, and the idea of her having a sister had absolutely thrilled her.

"Yes, she made it okay." Jeff found it difficult to keep his voice casual.

"Do you think you can get her to change her mind? You know, about meeting me?" Kirsten asked anxiously. "I mean, I understand that she's probably a little uptight about us, but for goodness' sake, isn't she the least bit curious?"

Jeff drew in a sharp breath. Damn it anyway, he thought, watching his sister's hopeful expression. How can I explain Hannah's conditions to her. How can I make her understand when *I* don't understand?

He forced a reassuring smile. "Of course, Hannah's curious. But she has her reasons for not wanting to meet the family, and we have to respect them."

His resentment turned into out-and-out despair as he watched his sister sag dejectedly against the bed.

"Sure," Kirsten said grudgingly. "I guess you're right."

"Hey!" he exclaimed. "Hannah's a nice person. But she's probably coping with some heavy emotions herself right now. After she's been up here awhile, after she feels more comfortable with the situation, I'm sure she'll change her mind. Hang in there. Sometimes these things just take a little special handling."

Kirsten immediately brightened. "Okay, big bro. I'll leave things in your capable hands. But remember, I do want to meet her."

They spent another ten minutes talking. Kirsten barraged him with question after question about Hannah. By the time he'd said good-night and put the phone down, he was drained with the effort of keeping his anxiety from showing. He had no guarantee he could get Hannah to meet Kirsten. He'd certainly struck out so far. But then again, he thought as he made his way to the lobby, he hadn't really tried that hard.

Jeff's still depressed, Hannah thought as she watched him walk across the lobby in her direction. He looked even more down than when they'd left the doctor's office. Hannah bit her lip. She considered asking him to have dinner with her and then immediately discarded that idea as her stomach contracted with nausea. No, she couldn't face food. And from the look on his face, he probably wasn't hungry, either.

She smiled brightly as he approached. "Hi," she said quickly. "If you're not in a hurry, how about taking a little walk with me? There's supposed to be a great view from the top of that hill over there." She pointed to her left. "One of the nurses told me about it. I don't know about you, but after being cooped up all day, I could sure use some fresh air." Hannah cringed inside because she sounded so phony, but it was the best she could come up with at the moment.

Jeff was so distracted he didn't even look surprised. "Sure," he murmured, taking her arm and leading her toward the door. "Fresh air sounds good."

Neither of them spoke as they crossed the parking lot and started up the hill. She glanced at him and her heart sank further. Jeff's hands were jammed in the pockets of his jeans; beneath the lightweight jacket he wore, his shoulders slumped and even his footsteps seemed to thud heavily on the pavement. He hadn't looked her in the eye since meeting her in the lobby. As far as Hannah could tell, Jeff's spirits were sinking faster than the setting sun.

He took her elbow as they came to a busy intersection. But the gesture was automatic and impersonal. Wanting to comfort him, she reached over and sympathetically squeezed his fingers. He didn't appear to notice. His gaze was fixed straight ahead.

Embarrassed, she pulled her hand away. It occurred to her that maybe he was so depressed, nothing could cheer him. But she hid her trepidation behind a bright smile as the light changed and they crossed the busy street.

"Was Kirsten feeling all right?" she asked cautiously.

He didn't answer till they reached the sidewalk, then he stopped and stared at her for a moment. "She's doing as well as can be expected," he replied, unconsciously parroting the phrase the medical staff used.

"Well, uh, that's good." Unable to stand his intense gaze, Hannah lowered her eyes and started walking. Oh, God, she thought morosely, what had she gotten herself into? Why did she think she had the ability to comfort this man? She barely knew him. She peered at him from beneath her lowered lashes. He was staring vacantly ahead.

Hannah swallowed nervously and wondered what to say next. A jogger trotted up behind them and she brushed against Jeff to give the runner room to pass. She had to do something. If Jeff's face tightened any more, it would crack.

For his part, Jeff was more frustrated and dejected than he'd been since Kirsten was diagnosed. He was gripped by a cold fear that had flared to life as he'd listened to the doctor's depressing assessment of his sister's chances.

Logically he knew Dr. Trevisi would be guilty of the worst kind of cruelty to offer them false hope, but hearing it spelled out so clearly to Hannah had opened up a lot of old wounds. Feelings he thought he'd come to terms with months ago were suddenly clamoring for release.

And seeing Kirsten had only made it worse. Her eagerness to meet her sister was like throwing water on a drowning man. As they reached the crest of the hill, he stopped beneath the streetlight and turned to look at Hannah.

Her jacket was unbuttoned, her hair was wind-blown and her face was flushed from the climb. Panting slightly, she stared at the panoramic view of the city. A gust of wind slammed into them and as he watched, he could see a nipple pucker against the thin fabric of her blouse. The sun had gone, but even in the deepening twilight he could see her body responding to the cool air.

He clenched his teeth as a flare of sensual excitement rippled through his body. Hell, he thought in disgust, dragging his gaze away from her breasts. Even under these awful circumstances I can't control my hormones. "Seen enough?" He winced at the harshness of his voice.

Hannah shrugged one shoulder. "I really wasn't interested in the view," she said honestly, turning to face him. "I just thought you might like some company. You looked pretty down after we left the doctor's office."

Surprised, he was taken aback. Either Hannah was incredibly perceptive or he'd unknowingly lowered his guard around her in a way that he didn't with anyone else. He was damned good at hiding his feelings. Normally he didn't let anyone see how badly he felt about his sister's illness.

"Yes, I was down when we left the office," he confessed. "I'd just been reminded in the most graphic terms of how very lousy my kid sister's chances really are." *And then I had to go and make excuses about why you don't want to meet her, he added silently.* But Jeff hurriedly stifled that resentful notion. Hannah was doing enough for them, and he had no right to expect anything more.

Hannah flushed. She felt a little foolish. "I thought maybe you'd want to talk it out with someone," she said lamely.

Jeff's eyebrows rose. "What's there to say?" he asked wearily. He ran a hand through his hair and closed his eyes for a brief moment. "You heard what the doctor said—'no guarantees.'"

Ridiculously she was hurt by his abruptness. Hannah stared at him for a moment and then looked down. She felt tears pool in her eyes but she blinked them back. "I'm sorry," she said, lifting her chin proudly. "I was only trying to help. But obviously, it's not something you want to discuss, and my efforts to cheer you up don't seem to be doing much good."

Jeff sighed heavily and slumped against the lamp-post. "It's very kind of you to be concerned. I appreciate your motives, I really do."

An awkward silence fell between them. Hannah fiddled with the buttons on her jacket and then cleared her throat. "Was Kirsten in a lot of pain?" she asked, trying to understand his mood. "Is that why you're so depressed?"

He ignored the last part of her question. "Kirsten's in no more pain than usual."

Hannah sucked in her breath as an image—one she'd pushed to the back of her mind years ago—rose up to haunt her. Mrs. Webster's pain-racked body in the last days of her illness flashed through her mind. But at least Kevin's mother had been at home. Poor Kirsten was stuck in an isolation ward. "I'm so sorry," she whispered, her voice shaky. Her eyes filled with tears again and this time she was afraid she couldn't keep them inside. Hastily she swiped at her cheek.

Jeff felt like a complete jerk. It wasn't Hannah's fault that Kirsten was ill. She was trying her best to help him and he was acting like a sulking two-year-old.

He reached over and grabbed her hand. "Please don't apologize," he said urgently. "I'm the one who's sorry. I shouldn't have let you see me like this."

"It's okay," she sniffed. She pulled her hand from beneath his and swiped at her eyes again. "I understand."

"God, I'm sorry, Hannah," he persisted, suddenly desperate to make her understand what had been driving him. "But hearing the truth about Kirsten's chances spelled out like that really shook me. It always does." He paused. "I guess I haven't accepted the situation as well as I've been pretending. Sometimes the pain builds inside me until it explodes. But usually, when I'm like this, I've got enough sense not to inflict myself on other people."

"Don't apologize," she countered swiftly. "You've got every right to feel lousy. You're not made of iron and you didn't inflict yourself on me—I invited you for a walk. Besides," she assured him, "I think I know how you feel."

He smiled faintly but didn't say anything.

Hannah hesitated for a brief moment and then plunged ahead before she lost her courage completely. "The reason I wanted to talk to you was so that I could tell you that things really are going to be all right. The transplant is going to be a success. Kirsten's going to make it. I know it. I can feel it in my bones." She surprised herself with the strength of her belief.

Jeff looked doubtful. "Do you really believe that? Or are you still just trying to cheer me up?"

She smiled. "I know so. Look, I'll admit it's a wonder I'm compatible with Kirsten. But don't you see? That's the real beauty of this whole situation. It was almost a miracle. And you've got to believe in it and keep on believing. If not for your sake, at least for Kirsten's.''

Some of the despair left Jeff's eyes. ''You really mean what you're saying, don't you?''

''Yes,'' she confessed. ''You know my father was a Presbyterian minister. I'm not as religious as he or my mother, but the one thing he did teach me that I really believe is that God does work in mysterious ways. And you've got to have faith in Him. Every time I was depressed or worried about something, Dad used to say, 'Hannah Leigh, God gave us a soul and a brain. He expects us to use them both.' ''

Jeff smiled wryly. ''I hate to be dense, but I don't think I see how that applies in my sister's case.''

''Don't you see?'' Hannah cried passionately. ''It's as plain as the nose on your face. Twenty-five years ago, Kirsten wouldn't have had a chance at all. But medical researchers used their collective brains and came up with the weapons to fight leukemia. And you've got to believe that God wanted me here. He gave me tissue compatible with my half sister's.'' Hannah broke off and took a deep breath. ''If that's not a message, Jeff, I don't know what is.''

Jeff stared at her for a long moment and then broke into a wide smile. He felt as though she'd suddenly reached out and taken half his burden from him. She looked so determined, so committed, that her optimism was irresistible. Surprisingly she had the power to make him believe there was hope, too.

They stared at each other for a long moment and then she shyly asked, ''Did you tell Kirsten I was here? Did that make her feel any better?''

For a moment, Jeff was tempted to tell her the truth. But he decided to wait a few minutes and lead up to it gradually. He had to handle things very delicately. If Hannah realized how desperate her family was not only to meet her but to have a relationship with her, it might scare her off completely.

"I told her and yes, the news did cheer her up." He suddenly grinned. "Kirsten's very curious about you. She asked a lot of questions. She wanted to know what you looked like, how tall you were, what color of hair you have. Things like that." Jeff paused fractionally and then smoothly said, "But she does want to meet you."

Hannah's smile vanished and he instantly retreated. "I haven't forgotten our agreement," he said reassuringly. "Besides, as the doctor said, she's in isolation. She couldn't meet you now, anyway, so I stalled her off. But—" he sighed "—I haven't figured out how to tell her she isn't going to meet you at all. I don't want to depress her."

Guilt knifed through Hannah. She hadn't thought about how her rules might affect Kirsten's mental state. She'd only considered her mother. "Oh, God," she said miserably, "I hadn't thought of that."

"Don't worry," Jeff said. "We'll think of something when the time comes. You're doing enough for us right now. I don't want you feeling guilty on top of everything else."

Yet Jeff couldn't help but wonder exactly why Hannah was so adamant about staying away from Kirsten and Irene. He wasn't going to push her. He'd meant it when he told Kirsten they had to respect Hannah's wishes, but he wasn't giving up, either.

Feeling relieved, Hannah smiled.

"But I'll admit, I am curious." Jeff cocked his head to one side. "Why don't you want to meet her? Aren't you in the least bit curious about her or Irene?"

Hannah bit her lip. She toyed with the idea of telling Jeff the truth. But that wouldn't be fair to Mary. To an outsider, her mother's fears would seem childish and selfish. No one who hadn't gone through the kind of devastating experience her mother had all those years ago could possibly understand Mary's emotional scars.

"Jeff," she began slowly, "I know you'll find this hard to believe, but I do have my reasons. Good reasons. But I'm not the only one involved and...they're complicated and personal."

He was tempted to press the point, but he could tell by the tone of her voice he'd pressed hard enough for one evening. "Why don't we change the subject?" he said lightly as he took her arm and started down the hill. "Let's talk about you."

"What do you want to know?" she murmured absently, turning her head to gape at a beautifully restored Victorian house.

"You never told me if you were involved with anyone."

The question unsettled her. Her head snapped around and she stumbled. Jeff's grip tightened on her arm. "I have a fairly active social life, and I date." She didn't add that her "social life" for the past fourteen months had consisted mainly of taking her mother out to dinner and helping at church bake-sales.

"You still haven't answered my question."

"Why do you want to know?" She tried to laugh, to make the question sound light, but she didn't pull it off.

Jeff could hardly admit that he wanted to know if she was available; if he would be poaching on another man's territory. That would sound too crass, and it wasn't the way he meant it. "Curiosity, I suppose. You've got to realize, Hannah, you're a beautiful young woman, and on a moment's notice you've dropped everything to help virtual strangers. I guess I'm just plain nosy."

Hannah felt a twinge of disappointment. Against her own better judgment, one part of her hoped he might be interested because he was *interested*. Don't be ridiculous, she told herself firmly. The last thing you need or want is to get romantically involved with Jeff Kenyon.

"You're hardly strangers," she replied. "And anyone would if they could."

Satisfied, Jeff smiled. Hannah wasn't involved with a man. The way she'd evaded the question had told him that much.

His optimism grew as they walked across the hospital parking lot. By the time he'd settled Hannah into his car and driven back to her motel, his confidence was fully restored.

Hannah stopped by the stairs leading to her room. "You don't have to walk me to my door," she said. "I'm sure you want to get home."

"Not at all," he replied, taking her hand and leading her up the steps. "And my mother taught me that a gentleman always sees a lady to her door."

The grip of his fingers sent a ripple of sensual pleasure through her body. She shivered as his touch made every nerve ending she had sit up and take notice. The roughness of his callused palms rubbing against her own sent a wicked thrill up her spine. She caught her

breath at the erotic image the slight friction was causing. His touch had the power to hurl a shock wave of
sensation all the way to her toes. She dropped his hand
and hastily fumbled in her purse for her key.

Protectively Jeff moved his hand to the small of her
back. Hannah almost moaned out loud. It wasn't fair.
Why was it this man? Even through her blouse and
jacket, his touch was searing her all the way to her
bones.

Mercifully they came to her room. Hannah unlocked the door, hit the light switch and stepped inside. "Thank you for the ride back," she said politely.

Jeff leaned against the door frame. "No, I'm the
one who should be thanking you. You were absolutely right. I did need to talk tonight." He stepped
closer and gazed into her eyes.

Hannah's throat went dry at the expression on his
face. The pale light from the top of the porch ceiling
cast shadows upon the angles of his cheekbones and
forehead, etching his face with stark, brooding lines—
except for his eyes. They were brilliant, opaque, and
glittering with desire.

Against her will, something inside her responded to
the mesmerizing blue heat reaching across the tiny
space that separated them. She balled her hands into
fists and went perfectly still as a jolt of erotic tension
arced between them. His desire was as sharp as the
blast of a dry Santa Ana wind against her bare skin.
The air sizzled with sudden heat.

Jeff's hands closed over her shoulders and he drew
her closer. He bent his head and brushed the gentlest
of kisses against her lips. At the touch of his mouth to
hers, what was left of her resolve crumbled com-

pletely. Sighing softly, Hannah twined her arms around his neck and relaxed against him.

That was all the encouragement he needed. The kiss grew wilder, hungrier, as Jeff thrust his tongue inside her mouth and pulled her tightly against him. He could feel the softness of her breasts against his chest. Her sweet scent filled his nostrils and his hands slipped from her shoulders and stroked her back as his tongue began to stroke rhythmically against hers.

Hannah was lost. She burrowed closer to him and dug her fingers into the soft hair behind his neck. At every contact point on her body the pressure rose, contracting her nerve endings and demanding a release. He tasted like wild honey and coffee; he tasted like the essence of life itself.

The specter of death had taken its toll on Hannah, too. Instinctively her body arched against his, seeking his warmth—his life. Her need was sudden, powerful and frightening.

One of his hands slipped around her ribs and closed over her breast. The sensation was exquisite. Her nipple hardened before his thumb even touched her. She gasped as he made contact with her flesh.

Jeff pulled away from her mouth and buried his lips at the base of her neck. She felt so good in his arms; so warm, so alive. And he needed her so much. Every muscle tensed in anticipation. He started kissing her throat, mumbling to her between the tiny, nibbling bites. Like a fool, he said the wrong thing: "Ah, Hannah, thank God we found you. You have no idea of what this means to me, to all of us. No matter what happens, no matter what the outcome, we'll always be grateful."

Hannah felt as though a bucket of cold water had just been dumped on her. She went rigid. It took a moment before Jeff felt her withdrawal. He stared down at her in surprise.

Avoiding his eyes, she stepped quickly out of his arms and sagged against the door. "We shouldn't do this," she told him breathlessly. "You'd better leave."

"What's wrong? What did I do?" He took a step toward her, his arms outstretched. But she moved away from him.

"You didn't do anything," she lied. "But we can't do this. We don't even know each other."

He took a deep breath. "I feel like I know you."

Hannah shook her head quickly. She was terrified. If she didn't get rid of him soon, they'd be in each other's arms in the blink of an eye. God knows, once he touched her she'd be lost. "No," she blurted out, "this isn't a good idea. I can't afford to get involved with you. There are too many problems. And besides, it isn't right. We were both just reacting to the depressing news we heard in the doctor's office."

Jeff raised his eyebrows skeptically and crossed his arms over his chest. "Do you think I'd have kissed anybody the way I just kissed you because I was depressed? I've been living with this fight for over two years now. I'll admit I was upset earlier, but take my word for it, I kissed you because I wanted to. And you responded for the same reason."

She started to say something, but he held up his hand. "Let's not kid ourselves. This isn't the end of this. There's something between us, and you know it."

Before she could open her mouth to tell him he was wrong, he'd stepped out the door and quietly pulled it closed.

Chapter Seven

Stunned, Hannah stared at the door for a good thirty seconds. A flicker of hope flared to life as his last words echoed through her mind. *There's something between us, and you know it.*

In a daze she stumbled to the bed and collapsed. She cringed as she realized how badly she wanted to believe Jeff; how badly she wanted to take his words at face value and actually be convinced there was something real between them—something that wasn't just gratitude and lust. But she couldn't do it. She couldn't allow herself to indulge in that kind of dangerous fantasy.

She wrapped her arms around herself as a whirlpool of conflicting emotions caught and held her tightly in the center of a swirling storm. One part of her urged her to take a chance, to see what would happen if she gave in to her overwhelming desire for

him, while another part whispered that she was a fool.
Jeff didn't even know her. How could he possibly care
for her? And maybe, the voice whispered slyly, maybe
if he gets to know you, he'll do the same thing Kevin
did.

Shuddering, Hannah forced her mind to go blank.
She climbed off the bed and walked slowly to the
bathroom. Mechanically she washed her face, brushed
her teeth and changed into her nightgown. By the time
she was ready for bed, she was utterly exhausted.

But sleep wouldn't come. She tossed and turned for
an hour before she finally faced what was bothering
her about Jeff's explosive kiss.

Gratitude. She smiled bitterly in the darkness. No
wonder she couldn't allow herself to have any faith in
his words. Even in the grip of passion, Jeff hadn't
been able to be anything less than honest: he'd gone on
and on about how damned grateful he'd always be.

Just like Kevin. Hannah sighed heavily. If it didn't
hurt so much, she'd have laughed at the ironies of fate.
Who would have thought that twice in a lifetime she'd
be involved with men who were grateful? Throw in a
little lust, she reflected cynically, and you've got the
makings of a real tearjerker here.

Deliberately Hannah forced herself to remember.
Only by reminding herself of the past would she have
the strength to resist Jeff. She closed her eyes and let
the once-painful memories wash over her.

She'd been nineteen and too madly in love to realize that Kevin hadn't returned her feelings. He'd just
been *grateful*.

For six months, she'd had a crush on him. She could
still vividly recall watching him out of the corner of
her eye when she was supposed to be listening to one

of her father's sermons. Kevin always sat across the aisle, next to his mother, and most of the time he was peeking back at her.

When he'd finally asked her out and they'd begun dating, she'd been on cloud nine. Both of them were enrolled in the same junior college and they had a lot in common. At the time, Hannah had convinced herself it was a match made in heaven. She'd been blindly, blissfully happy. And like a fool, she'd assumed Kevin was, too.

Then Anna Webster was struck with a terminal illness.

Hannah was passionately in love with Kevin and wanted to help him, so she'd thrown herself into nursing the woman she thought was going to be her mother-in-law.

As she and Kevin worked together nursing his mother, Hannah convinced herself their love was growing stronger with each passing day. She even rearranged her class schedule so Kevin wouldn't have to drop out of school. She'd spent every spare minute at the Webster house—cooking, cleaning, changing sheets, reading to Anna and making sure she got her medicine. But Anna had finally died.

The months passed and Hannah began to notice that Kevin never talked about their future together. He seemed to need a great deal of time alone. At first she thought he was grieving; after all, they were practically engaged and she trusted him. But when she finally confronted him about her feelings, he confessed that he didn't love her. He was eternally grateful for all she'd done, but he'd fallen in love with another woman and he hoped Hannah understood.

Staring up at the ceiling, Hannah renewed her vow to stay away from Jeff. Oh, he was attracted to her, all right—just as she was attracted to him. But she wasn't stupid enough to make the same mistake twice in one lifetime.

The first time had almost killed her. She'd been shattered. It had taken months to get her life back together. Months of wondering what she'd done wrong, how she could have so totally misunderstood the situation between herself and Kevin. Not only was she crushed, but she'd felt like a fool.

And Kevin's rejection had secretly affirmed a dread she'd been fighting all of her life: Hannah felt flawed.

The feeling was irrational, and logically, she knew it wasn't true. But she couldn't help it. From the moment she really understood what being adopted meant, that frightened-little-child part of her became convinced there was something horribly wrong with her— something so terrible that even her own mother had given her away rather than cope with it.

Deeply buried, the reawakened fear gnawed at her for months. Finally in desperation she'd thrown herself back into her schoolwork and finished her degree in record time.

Hannah had sworn she'd never mistake gratitude for love again.

Jeff wouldn't understand. To Hannah, gratitude was like a powerful, malevolent spirit. It could twist the mind into believing illusions and trick the heart into making foolish commitments. And when the crisis was past, Jeff would be the one to come to his senses, but she'd be the one left with a shattered life.

Not again.

* * *

He who hesitates is lost. The saying flashed into Jeff's mind as he hovered in front of Hannah's motel-room door.

Driven by the knowledge that if he didn't keep the pressure on, Hannah would disappear from their lives the minute the transplant was over, Jeff took a deep breath and rapped lightly against the wood.

He was determined not to lose. There was too much at stake for him to give up without a fight. He wouldn't let her just walk away. Kirsten and Irene needed her too much. *He* needed her.

Over the noise of the street traffic, he strained to hear the soft thud of her feet crossing the carpet or the slam of the bathroom door. When he heard nothing, he scowled in frustration and leaned over to peer in through the curtains.

The glare of the morning sun made it difficult to see, but by squinting, he was able to make out the faint glow of a bedside lamp. Jeff knocked again, louder this time.

A shaft of unease speared through him but he shrugged it off. He knew he was violating her terms by offering her a ride to the hospital. He didn't care. It was one of the few legitimate reasons he had for seeing her, for trying to understand why she was so adamant about staying away from them.

The door opened and Hannah appeared.

She was dressed. Jeff reacted automatically, his mouth curving appreciatively over the delightful picture she made. Staring at him with those huge brown eyes of hers, she wore a silky green blouse and figure-hugging black slacks. Her hair was loose and hanging in soft curls around her shoulders. A hairbrush dangled from her right hand.

She gasped on seeing him. Her tongue darted out and she licked her lips.

Jeff's gaze focused on her mouth. He remembered how she'd tasted, how she'd responded to him, and his blood quickened.

Correctly interpreting the hungry look in his eyes, Hannah stared at him for a moment and then blushed.

Jeff quickly brought himself under control and smiled politely. "I thought I'd give you a ride to the hospital."

"Oh, you didn't have to do that," she said. "I was going to call a cab."

"Now that I'm here, you can ride with me and save yourself fifteen bucks."

"But I don't want you going out of your way. This is a lot of trouble for you." Hannah nervously clutched the hairbrush to her chest.

"It's no trouble at all," Jeff countered, crowding a little closer toward her and forcing her back a step. "And it's not out of my way. I go to see Kirsten every morning on my way to work."

"But Jeff…" She frowned and looked down at her feet, not knowing how to voice her protest. How could you tell a man he made you giddy? That the very sight of him filled you with fear and excitement and snapped your pulse rate into double time? And he was just being polite. Grateful.

Jeff glanced at his watch and lifted his gaze to meet hers. A faint frown formed on her forehead and she chewed her lower lip. Seeing her indecision, he seized the offensive. "Your appointment's in half an hour. We don't have time to argue. Grab your purse and let's go. Take my word for it, giving you a ride is no big deal." He paused and grew serious. "It's the least I can do."

His words sent remorse flooding through her and she winced. It would be petty to refuse a lift. People needed to feel they could repay you in some small way when they accepted your help. No one liked to be obligated; her work at the community center had taught her that. Hannah expelled a long breath and weighed her options carefully. "All right. I'll just be a second."

Leaning against the door frame, Jeff waited as she walked to the dressing table and picked up her purse. He was pushing her and he knew it. But as long as he could cover his actions beneath the civilized mask of courtesy, she couldn't accuse him of violating their agreement.

On the drive to the hospital, Jeff politely played tour guide by pointing out Nob Hill and other spots of interest.

By the time they parted in the lobby, Hannah was almost relaxed. Jeff didn't mention seeing her again. She watched him disappear into the elevator, conscious of a twinge of disappointment that he hadn't offered her a ride back to her motel. But remembering her vow of the night before, she shook off the ridiculous notion and headed for her first appointment.

For the rest of the day, Hannah had a lot of time to think. There wasn't much else to do as she waited for one doctor after another to examine her. By the time she was ready for the last of the day's blood tests, she was unaccountably anxious. A vague sense of foreboding had crept into the back of her mind and made her as jumpy as a long-tailed cat in a roomful of rocking chairs.

Hannah sat up straighter in her seat and took a deep breath. She closed her eyes and forced herself to analyze the feeling nagging at the back of her mind. With a start, she realized what was wrong. It was Jeff. He wanted her to meet Kirsten and Irene.

Hannah sighed heavily. Of course. How could she have been so blind? How could she not have realized what the man was after? Her eyes flew open and she smiled cynically.

Jeff hadn't said anything straight out; she'd give him credit for that. But it was suddenly as clear to her as the headlines in the morning paper. Every time he mentioned either Irene or Kirsten, it was there, written as plain as day on his face. Oh, he was good! she thought grudgingly. Those beautiful blue eyes of his were as innocent as a newborn babe's. He was a master at hiding his feelings. But he wasn't quite good enough, and her subconscious had picked up on it.

She could see it now. There was a waiting quality about him. It was in his body language and in his eyes and in the way he watched her so closely whenever Kirsten's or Irene's name was mentioned. Jeff was stalking her and biding his time.

"Could you please roll up your sleeve."

The nurse's soft voice startled her. Hannah gave the young woman a brief smile and dutifully obeyed. She turned her head away as the nurse peeled the paper off the disposable needle.

The awful thing was, she was beginning to sympathize with Jeff's position. He was too decent a man to be playing games with her. And she knew she wasn't misinterpreting the signals her subconscious was sending her.

Hannah gasped as she felt a sharp prick in the crook of her arm. But the pain wasn't totally physical; it was emotional, too.

Jeff was sending her the clearest possible message: Kirsten needed her. And she was ignoring him, pretending not to understand. Deep inside, a tiny seed of guilt blossomed into full flower.

"There, now," the nurse said cheerfully as she plastered a bandage on the inside of Hannah's elbow. "That wasn't so bad. You're all done now. But we'll need another sample tomorrow morning. Make sure you don't eat or drink anything before the test."

Hannah leaped to her feet. No, she thought morosely as she snatched up her purse and bolted for the door. Today's tests hadn't been bad for her, but after being poked, prodded and subjected to a variety of physical indignities in the form of a complete physical, she could now imagine the kind of ordeal Kirsten went through every day of her life. The thought made Hannah feel wretched.

Today, the reality of Kirsten's illness had hit her like a bolt of lightning. Hannah paused by the door of the lab and glanced back over her shoulder. She drew a ragged breath as her gaze traveled slowly around the room.

Sunlight glittered off the stainless-steel medical instruments, the air was filled with the smell of wood alcohol and disinfectant, and from the hall, she could hear the sound of wheelchairs and gurneys moving patients from one place to another. This was a war zone and the enemy they were fighting was death.

Hannah winced. She could no longer distance herself from the pain.

It's not enough, she thought, turning and shoving open the door. I have to do more. A ripple of fear shot up her spine as she realized what she was thinking, but she determinedly pushed it aside.

She could no longer pretend she was just doing a good deed. The need to get involved, to offer what aid and comfort wherever she could, clawed at her insides and clamored to be let out.

Fighting for one's life was sheer hell, and Kirsten did it every day. Hannah felt guiltier than ever.

All the way down in the elevator, she pondered what to do next. Maybe it wouldn't hurt to meet Kirsten? Maybe it would help the girl.

As she emerged from the elevator, Hannah spied the trio on the other side of the lobby and she halted so abruptly, the nurse behind her bumped into her.

Hannah barely noticed. She forgot to breathe and her heart almost stopped in her chest. Jeff was huddled in conversation with a man and woman. It had to be the Kenyons. Hannah couldn't take her eyes off the woman. Irene Kenyon.

Her mother. Her birth mother.

Jeff looked up and glanced quickly around the lobby.

Hannah's breath caught in her throat, her ears were ringing, and she thought for a moment she might faint. She didn't want him to see her. Her luck held, because his glance flicked past her without a hint of recognition. She slipped behind a pillar.

Irene Kenyon was lovely, Hannah thought. Medium height, perfectly coifed ash-blond hair, and she was dressed in an aqua-blue pantsuit that showed off her slender figure to perfection. Except for the worried expression in her brown eyes, she was the very picture of a well-to-do society matron.

Irene reached across and touched Jeff's arm. She seemed almost to be pleading. Jeff shook his head and smiled sadly. Hannah's stomach plummeted. Dear God, Hannah wondered frantically, was there something wrong with Kirsten? Another problem on top of the ones they already had?

Her throat went dry and a knot of apprehension tightened in her chest. For one crazy moment she fought the impulse to run across the floor and demand that they tell her what was going on. But she caught herself before she'd taken the first step.

Reece Kenyon, as tall and handsome as his son, threw his arm over his wife's shoulders and gently guided her toward the main door.

Hannah slumped against the pillar. Sympathy welled up in her and left her gasping for air. The room suddenly seemed devoid of oxygen and it hurt to breathe. Hannah gulped and swallowed to ease the pain in her chest. Several moments passed before she got her emotions under control. Then she walked slowly across the lobby toward Jeff.

She no longer cared that he was maneuvering her into meeting Kirsten and Irene. That particular worry had faded the minute she'd seen the anxious way the three of them had been grouped together. She had to know what was going on; she had to know if Kirsten was all right.

Jeff didn't notice her till she was standing next to him. Hannah touched his arm.

"Oh, hi." He smiled distractedly. "How did it go today?"

"Fine," she assured him with a bright, fake smile. "Mind you, I got the impression they're a blood-thirsty lot around this place. Every time I turned around, they were draining more out of me." She deliberately tried to make a joke of everything. She didn't want him guessing she'd just had one of the most traumatic moments of her life.

Jeff smiled again, but it didn't go anywhere near his eyes. He was genuinely worried, and the lump in her chest contracted in fear. "How's Kirsten?" she asked.

He shrugged. "She's hanging in there." Absently he raked his hand through his hair and shifted toward the door.

Terrified he was going to leave without telling her anything, Hannah impulsively tugged on his arm again. "Can you give me a ride back to the motel?"

Startled, he looked down at Hannah's hand. "Sure."

But try as she might, she couldn't get him to open up. Hannah could hardly admit she'd been hiding behind a pillar and spying on him and his parents. So she buried her questions cleverly in casual conversation. But that didn't work, either; Jeff spent the entire drive playing tour guide again.

Hannah was wild with frustration by the time they pulled into the parking lot of the motel. Grimly she determined to find out what was going on if it took her all night. If she didn't know better, she'd almost swear Jeff knew what she was trying to do and was deliberately being evasive. Obviously subtlety was lost on the man.

But she had another surprise waiting for her when she got out of the car.

The desk clerk stuck his head out of the office. "Miss Breckenridge!" he called. "Oh, Miss Breckenridge. Your luggage is in here." He grinned cheerfully and ducked back inside the office.

Hannah gaped at the disappearing clerk for a moment and then flew across the lot, with Jeff trailing behind her.

"What's my luggage doing in here?" she demanded as she threw open the door and saw her suitcases neatly stacked in the corner.

The clerk stared at her in surprise, his watery blue eyes turning suspicious. "But Miss Breckenridge," he explained slowly, "I told you the day you checked in, the room was only available for two nights. Don't you remember?"

"What?" She bit her lower lip and tried to recall what the clerk had said when she checked in. All she could remember was that she'd been so distracted she could barely write her address.

"We're booked solid for the next two weeks. I told you." He picked up a racing form from the counter. "The whole town's filled with conventions."

"Oh, my God. Are you saying I don't have a room for tonight?"

"That's exactly what he's saying, Hannah," Jeff interjected dryly. He walked over to the pile of luggage. Picking up a suitcase with each hand, he said, "Settle your bill while I get these to the car. And don't look so worried. You won't have to sleep on the streets tonight." Jeff pushed the door open and called back over his shoulder. "We'll go back to my place and you can call around and find another room."

Hannah had no choice. She paid her bill and hurried out to his car.

* * *

Jeff's apartment was located in a multistory stucco building at the top of a hill. Hannah gave a long, low whistle as she gazed at the fabulous view of the city and the bay. "My gosh, this is incredible!" she exclaimed, getting out of the car and turning slowly to take it all in. "Hey, look! There's the Golden Gate Bridge."

"I know," Jeff said dryly. He opened the trunk and pulled out her bags. "It's there all the time."

Hannah laughed. "I must sound like a real tourist," she began, her voice faltering as she saw the suitcases. "Why are you getting my bags out?"

"So you'll have them to take to a hotel." He picked a bag up with each hand and started for the door. "In the past five years I've lost a set of golf clubs, two radios and a fifty pound box of tools. Believe me, if you want to keep it, you don't leave it in the trunk of your car."

The interior of Jeff's apartment was attractive, cluttered, and filled with books. Hannah stared in amazement at the floor-to-ceiling bookcases lining two of the walls. A huge brick fireplace was at one end of the room and directly in front of her was a huge picture window with the same fantastic view she'd seen from the street.

She walked to a bookcase and lovingly ran her hand over a row of hardbacks. "This is a regular library."

"You've discovered my secret vice," Jeff said with a laugh. "Not only do I love to read, but I'm a pack rat, too. I can't resist garage sales, used-book stores or bargain basements." He grinned cheerfully, put her bags on the floor and tossed his car keys onto an oak end table next to the couch.

"The phone's in the den, through there." He nodded toward a hall leading off the living room. "Help yourself. I'm going to change and then we'll rustle up some steaks."

For the next half hour, Hannah made call after call. The story was the same everywhere. The only available room cost two hundred dollars a night, every reasonably priced place in town was booked solid. Sighing, she picked up the receiver one last time and dialed her mother.

Mary answered on the first ring. "Hello."

"Hi, Mom," Hannah said with forced cheer. "How are you?"

"I'm fine, dear, and I'm so glad you called. I was going to call you later tonight," she replied breathlessly.

"Why. Is everything all right?"

"Things are fine," Mary assured her. "But I did want you to know I'm going to be out of town for a few weeks."

"Out of town. You? Where are you going?"

She heard Mary take a deep breath.

"Mexico."

"What?" Hannah stared at the receiver.

"I'm going with Pastor McMahon," Mary explained in a rush. "Mrs. Hersheimer, our youth leader, fell and sprained her ankle. John and I are taking her youth group down to that orphanage outside of Mexicali. You remember, dear—the youth group goes every year. It's very important for teenagers to get a real chance to help people. And the associate pastor's been dying for a chance to have the pulpit all to himself."

Hannah's spirits soared. At least one of her worries seemed to be under control. Mary would be gone! She'd have something to keep her from fretting over her daughter. "That's terrific, Mom. I'm sure it'll be a wonderful experience. When do you leave?"

"That's why I was going to call you tonight, dear. I didn't want you to worry if you tried to phone me and I wasn't there." She laughed. "We're leaving at five, tomorrow morning."

Mary's excitement was contagious. By the time Hannah put the phone down she'd forgotten she was temporarily homeless.

Jeff came to the door. He'd changed into a pair of comfortable old jeans that molded to his long legs and lean hips, and a pale blue chamois-cloth shirt that brightened his eyes to a high-powered blue. "Find anything?"

It was hard not to stare, but Hannah managed it. She smiled wryly. "There's a possibility." She winced as she remembered the price she'd been quoted. "And if I get really desperate, there were at least two places that offered to charge by the hour."

He laughed. "Come on, let's get some dinner cooked and we'll try again later."

She rose and followed him down the short hall toward the kitchen. The room was like the rest of the apartment—contemporary and clean, but cluttered with newspapers, magazines and coffee mugs.

Jeff was pulling a package of steaks from the refrigerator. "There's potatoes in the microwave. I'll handle the steaks if you'll make the salad."

For an instant she hesitated and then walked over to the spot he'd just vacated and started digging in the crisper for lettuce and tomatoes. The intimacy of cooking together was suddenly frightening. But it was delicious, too—like the moment when one was poised at the top of the roller coaster. It was too late to get off and she didn't want to, anyway.

"How do you like your steak?" Jeff squatted in front of the grill and slid the meat off the plate and onto the broiler.

"Medium rare," she answered, her voice muffled by the sound of running water as she washed the vegetables.

"Good." He straightened. "That's how I like mine." He gazed thoughtfully at her back. Her mood was much lighter, and that gave him courage. Walking to the large oak table on the other side of the kitchen, he poured two glasses of wine.

"Here." He walked up behind Hannah and leaned forward to put the glass on the windowsill. His leg brushed the back of her thigh and his arm accidentally nudged the side of her breast. The contact was brief, but potent. He stepped back as though he'd been burned.

"Thanks." She shook the lettuce. "Was everything all right with Kirsten today? You seemed distracted earlier."

Hannah decided that enough was enough. She wanted to know if Kirsten was all right, and she was tired of playing games.

Jeff hid a smile behind a sip of wine. He'd known she'd been pumping him—she'd tried to get him to talk all the way back to the motel. But he'd deliberately ignored her subtle probing. He wanted her to trust him enough to just ask him straight out.

When he didn't answer, Hannah turned and stared at him quizzically.

"Kirsten's fine," he replied hastily. "But naturally, we worry. So I guess you must have picked up on that."

"Oh." She nodded and began tearing the outer leaves off the lettuce. "Can you get me a bowl?"

Jeff reached into a cupboard, pulled down a wooden bowl and set it on the counter next to the sink.

He wondered if he should mention Irene. His stepmother had been nearly frantic tonight at the hospital. She was almost beside herself with fear that Hannah would never want to meet her. It had taken both him and Reece ten minutes to calm her down.

"Do you want onions?"

"Huh? Oh, sure." Jeff walked back to the stove and hunkered down to check the steaks. "Now, about your bed for the night."

Hannah opened the drawer and pulled out a knife. She began slicing tomatoes. "I'm not too worried. There's a minisuite at Hartley's available. If I don't have any better luck after dinner, I'll take that for a few days."

"Good God, Hannah!" he exclaimed, staring at her in shock. "That place costs a fortune. You're not made of money. At least let me—" He broke off as she vigorously shook her head.

"It's all right, Jeff. I've told you. I want to do this." The tone of her voice warned him not to argue.

The aroma of sizzling meat wafted up from the broiler and Jeff flicked a quick look inside to make sure it wasn't burning. The germ of an idea was forming in his brain.

He stood up and watched her finish making the salad, noting the tiny curve of her lips and the happiness in her eyes. For some reason, she wasn't depressed or upset. As a matter of fact, her mood was lighthearted and her natural optimism was completely restored—not what you'd expect from someone facing a two-hundred-dollar-a-night hotel bill.

The microwave dinged and Hannah went to get the potatoes. Jeff served the steak and poured each of them more wine.

He stalled as they ate, talking about everything except what was uppermost in his mind. When Hannah finished off the last of her food, he dropped his bombshell.

"I've got an idea," he said. "There's no need for you to spend the kind of money Hartley's will charge."

"I'm not going to the No-Tell Motel where they charge by the hour, either," she announced with a grin. "And that's about all that's available."

"Of course not," he agreed, though actually the thought of Hannah and a hot-sheet motel sent his pulse rate soaring. "But there's an even better solution. One that's been right under our noses all along."

"What's that?" She smiled quizzically.

"You can stay with me."

Chapter Eight

Jeff was an expert negotiator. He'd faced irate truckers, screaming managers and presidents of steamship lines without breaking into a sweat. But it took every ounce of his willpower to keep his cool while he watched Hannah from across his own kitchen table. He wanted her to stay. Badly.

She'd gone perfectly still, her wineglass poised halfway to her parted lips, her brown eyes wide and wary. "You want me to stay here?" she asked in a stunned voice.

"Don't look so shocked," he said easily, giving her a reassuring smile. "I'm only suggesting you stay as my houseguest."

"You can't be serious." Nervously she moistened her lips and when she lowered the glass, her fingers trembled. "I can't stay here."

"Why not?"

"Why not?" Hannah repeated. "There's dozens of reasons."

"Name one."

"Jeff—" Her mind went blank. She couldn't think. Picking up her napkin, she twisted it into a tight ball as she frantically tried to come up with an answer.

"Well," she finally said, grabbing at the first thing that flew into her mind, "it would violate the agreement we made."

"I don't see how," Jeff replied casually, leaning back in his chair. He crossed his arms over his chest. "I'm not related to you. As I understand it, it's your birth relatives you want to avoid. Right?"

Hannah felt giddy. "Well, yes," she stammered hastily. "But...don't your parents ever come by? That would be awkward. I mean, I can't ask you to cut yourself off from your entire family just because I'm here."

Jeff refrained from pointing out that the simplest thing to do would be to meet them. Like any good negotiator, he preferred to postpone some issues until he had a firm commitment.

He smiled briefly. "That's no problem. I'll make sure Dad and Irene know you're here. I'd be lying if I said they didn't want to meet you, especially Irene. But they understand your terms and they're willing to respect your privacy."

She shifted nervously in her chair. He looked totally unconcerned about making things uncomfortable with his family. She wavered, thinking of the Kenyons.

Guilt gnawed at her like a baby with a teething ring. She knew they wanted to meet her, knew it would mean a lot to them. But she couldn't. It would be too disloyal to Mary. She'd promised her mother to stay away from her birth family; and even though Mary had claimed it didn't matter, it was still one promise Hannah intended to keep.

"It's not just that," she said slowly, racking her brain for an excuse that would convince not only him, but herself, as well. Because she was suddenly very tempted—more tempted than she'd ever been in her life. "For goodness' sake, you've got your own life to lead. I'd be in the way. Besides, we hardly know each other."

Jeff was determined to demolish every one of her objections. He shook his head. "I feel like I've known you a long time."

"But you haven't," Hannah protested. "And having a perfect stranger in your house is crazy. Especially now."

His brow wrinkled in a puzzled frown. "Why now?"

She dropped her gaze to the table and began tracing the grooves in the oak wood with her fingers.

"Well," she began hesitantly. "Right now you're under a lot of pressure, a lot of stress. You need your parents—and they need you." She raised her eyes to meet his. "You're facing an unbelievable ordeal. All of you need comfort and support. I can't ask you to keep your parents away because I'm staying here. It wouldn't be fair."

Jeff stared at her for what seemed an eternity. Faint lines of tension appeared around his mouth and his jaw tightened. He leaned forward, his eyes glittering like shards of blue ice. "You know," he said quietly, "you're absolutely right."

His ready agreement sent a flood of disappointment washing through her.

"I do need a lot of support right now," he continued in a low, soft voice. "And I need it from you."

Hannah's mouth fell open in amazement. "What?"

"Just being around you makes me strong, Hannah," he continued, ignoring her surprised expression. "Ever since Kirsten was diagnosed, I've been fighting this on my own. Dad and Irene were so shattered by the news that I was the one who had to take charge, had to be tough. I was the one who had to make all the decisions. I was the one who could never break down and let either of them see how damned scared and angry I was!"

Hannah's heart filled with compassion. She knew exactly what he'd been going through. She'd gone through the same thing after her father died. Mary hadn't been capable of anything but clinging to her. "Oh, Jeff, I know and I'm so sorry. A burden like this can be almost unbearable."

"I don't know what it is about you. Maybe it's your incredible optimism or maybe it's your strength. Or maybe it's because I let my feelings show around you in a way that I can't around my parents." He shook his head. "Whatever the reason, right now, you're the only one who can help me get through this. I need you, Hannah. Please stay."

Jeff suddenly realized he wasn't cutting a business deal or negotiating a lower rate with an independent trucker. Nor was he trying to get her to stay for his family's sake, either. He wanted her there for himself.

Hannah simply looked at him. He needed her with a desperation that touched her all the way to her soul.

She couldn't turn her back on him. She couldn't ignore his plea and say the one little word that would guarantee she could get back to San Diego with her heart intact. And she knew deep down inside that agreeing to stay with Jeff would be the biggest risk she'd ever taken.

Hannah drew a long, ragged breath. Of all the arguments he could have used to convince her, he'd found the one she couldn't refuse. "Well," she murmured, dropping her eyes away from his compelling gaze, "maybe it could work."

"Of course, it'll work," he insisted. "You'd save a ton of money and be a lot more comfortable than at a hotel. I guarantee you'll have all the privacy you need. I'm gone all day at work. Take a look around. This is a big apartment."

Hannah dutifully looked around.

"Besides," he said quickly, seeing her resolve begin to crumble. "It would only be for a few days, a week at the most."

She whirled back to face him, her eyes wide. "Does that mean we're ready for the transplant?"

"Dr. Trevisi told me that as soon as your tests check out, we'll go ahead. Kirsten's treatments are almost finished. She's as ready as she'll ever be."

"I don't know," she said hesitantly, but her voice lacked conviction. "I don't want to be in your way."

"You could never be in my way."

Hannah took a deep breath and came to a decision. As long as she remembered what motivated him, she'd be safe. As long as she kept reminding herself that all he really felt was gratitude, she'd be able to defend herself. Right now, he needed her strength and her optimism; but when it was over, he wouldn't need her anymore. It was a tricky situation, but she couldn't find it in her to say no. Not even to protect herself.

But there was one more thing she had to get straight.

Hannah cleared her throat. "I'm not sure how to say this, but if I stay . . ." She trailed off as she felt her cheeks turn pink.

"You want me to keep my hands to myself?" Jeff finished for her. He smiled enigmatically. "Don't worry. I'm well aware that there's an attraction between us. I'm equally aware that for some reason, you're determined not to let either of us take it any further."

"I think that's the wisest course of action," she said hastily. "Don't you agree?"

"No," he answered bluntly. "I'd like to give us a chance. But it's obvious you're not interested. And I don't push."

"Jeff," she said urgently, "I'm sorry. It's not what you think. But situations like this can be dangerous. They can fool people into thinking they feel things they really don't. And when it's over, both of us would end up hurt."

He gave her a long, appraising look. "Why are you so sure it would end?" he asked cautiously. "For goodness' sake, I don't routinely kiss women the way I kissed you last night. And you responded. There's something between us, and you know it."

"I'll admit I'm attracted to you," she said in a sudden burst of honesty. "But that's not enough. There's too many risks, too many reasons not to get involved. It wouldn't work out for either of us."

"Why not?"

"For one thing, we live four hundred miles apart."

"I'm in San Diego a lot on business. We could work something out."

"Jeff," she said impatiently, "that was only an example of the practical problems we'd face, let alone all the other reasons things could never work between us. Take my word for it. I'm doing us both a favor. There's no future in any kind of relationship between us."

"You can't see the future," he insisted, his voice serious. "You don't know what would happen if we gave ourselves a chance."

"But I *do* know," she declared. "I know exactly what would happen. Right now, you're seeing me as some kind of lifeline. And you're so damned grateful, you're convincing yourself you're genuinely interested in me. But you're not. And we'd both end up miserable if I let anything happen between us."

Jeff's jaw tightened. "Don't you think you're being just a bit arrogant? How do *you* know what I feel?"

Hannah felt cornered. "Because I've done this before!" she shouted. She snapped her mouth shut as she realized she was going too far, telling him too much. Taking a deep breath, she said, "Look, the only way I can stay here is if we both understand I'm just a houseguest."

"All right." He held up his hand in a placating gesture. He wanted to argue with her, to smash each and every one of her concerns. But he didn't want to risk losing her by having it out with her now. That could wait. "I want you here. If those are your terms, you've got my word. You'll be my houseguest and nothing else."

Turning a deaf ear on the screams coming from her common sense, Hannah smiled. "All right. We'll give it a try. But if I find it's not working out, I'll move to a hotel.''

Staying as Jeff's houseguest was easy. Except for loading the dishwasher and making her bed, she didn't even have to help with the housework. Mrs. Holiday, his cleaning lady, came in twice a week.

And Jeff was true to his word. Over the next few days he treated Hannah with the kind of courtesy usually reserved for a visiting maiden aunt.

Her medical tests were finished the morning after she moved into Jeff's spare bedroom, and she had several days to kill before the extraction procedure. They wouldn't take bone marrow from her until every single medical test had been analyzed and she was declared absolutely healthy.

Hannah toyed with the idea of flying to San Diego and checking in on the community center. She even called Jeremiah to see how things were going. But he assured her the center was getting along fine and reminded her that she hadn't taken any vacation time in two years.

So Hannah reluctantly became a tourist. She was too restless to sit around Jeff's apartment every day and she didn't know anyone in the city, so she forced herself to go from one tourist attraction to another.

She and Jeff quickly developed a routine. Every morning he'd fix them breakfast and then drop her off at the BART station on the way to the hospital for his morning visit with Kirsten.

Between the ultramodern rapid-transit system and the cable cars, Hannah saw every place of interest the city had to offer. She said a prayer for Kirsten at Grace Cathedral, climbed Nob Hill twice, strolled through every inch of Golden Gate Park, and fed the pigeons in Union Square.

By the time she got home in the evenings and let herself in with the key he'd given her, she was ready to drop.

Their first two evenings together, he insisted on taking her out to dinner. But after a couple of days of eating nothing but restaurant food, her stomach couldn't stand it anymore so she picked up some groceries on the way home from Ghirardelli Square. Jeff protested politely when he found her cooking in his kitchen, but after stuffing himself on her chicken and dumplings, he announced she was welcome to move in permanently if she'd do the cooking.

As she got to know Jeff, Hannah was alarmed to find that in this case, familiarity did not breed contempt. As they took the first tentative steps toward becoming friends, their basic attraction blossomed into something far more dangerous—at least for Hannah. Not only did she like the man, she was starting to admire him and, even worse, she found they had a lot in common.

They shared similar tastes in books, plays, music and films. Neither of them watched much television, but they were both news hounds and faithfully watched the national news every evening before dinner. Inevitably there was always some current issue that sparked an interesting debate between them that usually lasted through dinner and led off into dozens of different topics by the time they were loading the dishwasher.

But despite his being the perfect host and her striving to be the perfect houseguest, there was an undercurrent of tension between them.

Jeff had subtly raised the issue of her meeting Irene. But each time he mentioned it, Hannah had either ignored the question or found an excuse to leave the room.

But that wasn't the only thing causing the tension. They'd be clearing the dinner dishes or sipping a glass of wine in front of the fireplace when Jeff would fix his gaze on her with a hard, brilliant expression that had the power to send shivers up Hannah's spine. Or she'd glance up from a book and see him staring at her with a faint, almost predatory gleam, and against her will, every cell in her body would respond. Her pulse would sing and her stomach would tighten as the primitive, deeply female part of her recognized that look and positively gloried in it. He wanted her.

By the evening before the extraction, the tension between them had become so thick they were both at the snapping point.

Hannah couldn't pinpoint precisely when things began to come to a head, but looking back on it, it was probably when Jeff had picked her up in the hospital lobby late that afternoon.

The procedure of extracting her bone marrow was going to be done under a general anesthetic and she'd gone over to the hospital to pick up her instructions on what she could and could not eat or drink in the twelve hours preceding the process.

She and Jeff had arranged to meet in the lobby. But when the elevator doors had opened she'd spotted him standing with his parents by the front door. She'd quickly dodged behind a pillar, but this time, Jeff had seen her.

The drive home hadn't been pleasant. Both of them were anxious and preoccupied. Hannah pointed out that Jeff was driving too fast and he'd coolly informed her that he used to be a truck driver and knew what he was doing. But he did slow down.

Neither of them broke the taut silence as they entered his apartment. Hannah watched Jeff shrug off his suit coat and toss it carelessly onto the back of the couch.

Hannah dropped her purse on the couch as well. "Are you hungry?" she asked, determined to be civil.

"What?" Jeff's head snapped up. He shook his head as he loosened his tie. "No. Go ahead and make yourself something."

She was at home in his kitchen but she didn't take one step in that direction. Why was he so worried? she wondered. She was the one "going under the knife," so to speak. Kirsten wasn't scheduled to receive her marrow for several days. The extraction process was quite separate from the infusion process. But Jeff was definitely edgy. Come to think of it, she remembered, his parents had looked anxious, too. "Are your parents all right? Are they worried something might go wrong tomorrow?"

Jeff gave a short, harsh laugh. "Yeah, they're worried." His eyes narrowed. "Aren't you? Aren't you just the tiniest bit worried, Hannah? Or do you still believe in miracles?"

She gazed at him for a long moment, wondering at the sarcasm in his tone. "Of course, I'm worried. What's wrong with you? I just asked you a simple question."

"What's wrong?" he echoed incredulously. "All this wonderful concern about my family from a woman I saw hide behind a pillar rather than meet them face-to-face."

Hannah's breath caught and her hands clenched into fists. "I didn't hide behind a pillar, as you so crudely put it," she replied icily. "I merely waited till you were finished talking. Intruding into a private conversation isn't my idea of good manners. I was taught better than that. As for my concern, well, I assure you, if it's misplaced, I'll keep my mouth shut in the future."

He stared at her stonily. "You know," he said in a flat, even voice, "it would have meant a lot if you'd come over and let me introduce you to Irene. She's going through hell."

Hannah's nails dug deeply into her palms as guilt reared its ugly head. "I know that," she whispered. "You've all been going through hell. But I couldn't. I just couldn't."

"Why not?" He desperately needed to understand. Jeff looked at her, the expression on his face mirroring his confusion and his frustration.

"Jeff, we had an agreement."

"Oh, yes. I'm well aware of our agreement. But does it have to be carved in stone, Hannah? Can't you see how badly Irene needs you now? Can't you understand what meeting you would mean to her?" he beseeched.

An awful hollow feeling started in the pit of Hannah's stomach as she heard the desperate plea in his voice. Her hand flew to her mouth as pain slashed through her heart. Unable to stand the bleakness in his face, she dropped her gaze and stared at the floor. "I've got a good reason for the condition I've imposed," she said huskily. "And you have no right to try and change things at the last minute and make me feel guilty. You're not being fair."

"Fair? Is it fair that my seventeen-year-old sister is fighting for her life? Is it fair that my stepmother is half out of her mind with worry and her own daughter won't even say hello to her. Tell me what's fair, Hannah, and then maybe I can understand your reasons for withholding yourself from someone who needs you." His hands clenched into fists. "Make me understand, Hannah. Make me understand how someone who I know is a kind, compassionate human being can turn her back on her own mother and sister."

His words pierced her like a hot needle. "I've done what I can," she said defensively. "I've kept my part of the agreement. I'm donating my bone marrow."

"That's supposed to be enough?" He stared at her incredulously. "You just shell out a few ounces of bone marrow and walk away." Jeff shook his head in disbelief. He'd have bet his last dime that when Hannah knew, when she really knew how desperate Irene was to meet her, she'd give in. But he'd been wrong. And he didn't know why.

She couldn't take any more. "That's not true. I can't meet Irene and I can't meet Kirsten."

"Tell me why!" he thundered. "Make me understand!"

"Stop shouting!" Hannah yelled. She pushed a lock of hair out of her eyes and took a deep breath. "My mother," she explained breathlessly. "She couldn't handle it. You don't understand. I'm not being cruel to Irene. But I promised my mother I wouldn't have anything to do with my birth family."

His dark eyebrows drew together as he tried to make sense of what she was saying. "You promised your mother?"

Feeling like a traitor, Hannah clamped a hand over her mouth. She shouldn't have told him about Mary. Tears pooled in her eyes and she hurriedly brushed them away. "I'm sorry," she whispered. "But I can't meet Irene."

His shoulders slumped and he sighed heavily. "All right," he said with defeat in his voice. He stared at her through a red haze of despair and frustration. Irene's tearful plea in the hospital lobby flashed into his mind. *Please,* she'd begged, her eyes filled with pain, *ask Hannah if I can stop by tonight. I'd like to tell her how much this means to me. To all of us. Oh, God, Jeff. Tell her I need her!*

The torment in his stepmother's face had pushed him over the edge. He'd looked at the woman who'd loved him, raised him and become a mother to him, and he'd had to tell her no, Hannah wouldn't budge. She hadn't been prepared to discuss the issue once during the past five days. Every time he'd brought it up, she'd either changed the subject or fled to her room.

He'd spent the better part of a week restraining himself, trying to lull her into trusting him enough to let him get close. But it hadn't worked, and now he was faced with the risk of not only losing his sister, but losing Hannah, as well. It was more than he could stand at the moment.

Jeff raked her with one last, bleak look, turned his back and walked slowly down the hall to his bedroom.

Hannah stood frozen to the spot. A moment later, she heard the slam of his bedroom door. The resounding crash was enough to get her moving toward her own room.

She felt as though she were being torn in two. All she could think of was escape. She needed to run from the rage and the anguish and most of all, the guilt. Jeff's pleas were more than she could stand.

Hannah jerked her suitcase out from under the bed. She'd go to a hotel. Yes, that's what she'd do. There had to be an empty room somewhere, she thought as she flung the case onto the bed and popped it open.

Blinking back tears, she began to pack. Blinded by unshed tears, she didn't see Jeff standing in the open doorway until she slammed straight into his chest.

"What the hell do you think you're doing?" He glared at the open case. "Running out?"

Hannah blinked hard and refused to look at him. She focused on his top button. "I'm going to a hotel. I think that would be better for both of us. Don't worry, I'll be at the hospital tomorrow morning. Despite your accusations, I'm not running out."

Jeff sagged heavily against the door frame, his eyes staring at her flushed face. "I'm sorry."

"Forget it." She tried to move past him but he shifted quickly and blocked her exit. "It doesn't matter, anyway."

"It does matter," he insisted, reaching over and lifting her chin. He forced her to meet his gaze. "And I won't forget it. I'm sorry, Hannah. I had no right to push you."

"Didn't you?" she asked, searching his face.

"No," he said quietly. "Whatever your reasons are, I've got to respect them." Jeff closed his eyes for a brief moment and took a deep breath. "Forgive me. I'm half out of my mind with fear, and Irene's a basket case. But that doesn't give me the right to take it out on you."

Her anger faded. His eyes were filled with pain. Tears again flooded her own eyes and she swallowed to loosen the lump lodged in her throat. "It's okay," she whispered. "I understand. It's not all your fault. Believe me, I know what you're going through, what this situation is doing to you. I know how much pressure you're under. But I made a promise, Jeff. A promise to my mother. And I have to keep it."

They stared at each other silently. Then, with a ragged moan, Jeff pulled her close and buried his face in the curve of her shoulder.

Wanting to comfort him, Hannah lifted her arms around his neck and laid her head against his chest. She could feel the heavy beat of his heart in her ear, feel his ragged breath against the flesh of her neck.

"Oh, God, Hannah," he muttered hoarsely, "I'm so damned scared she's going to die!"

"No, no!" she protested, shaking her head fiercely and clutching him tighter. "You mustn't think that. You mustn't even say it. Kirsten won't die. I know it. You said it yourself—my being a match was almost a miracle. I know she'll be all right." She raised her head and looked at him, her expression pleading with him to believe her. "I just know it."

Jeff gazed into her eyes for a long moment and then pulled her close again. His hands stroked slowly up and down her back as they stood locked together, drawing comfort from each other.

Without thinking, Hannah began massaging the hard muscles on the backs of his shoulders. She closed her eyes and melted against him. She sighed as his clean, earthy scent drifted into her nostrils and filled her lungs. She felt his hands shift and move to the curve of her hips and pull her tighter against his loins. She gasped; he was aroused.

Her head began to spin as a flare of pure, hot desire broke free and spread like wildfire through her whole body. She moaned softly and tried to step back. Jeff wouldn't let her. Slowly he lowered his head until their lips touched.

The kiss was gentle at first, but within moments, they were ravenous for each other. Their tongues touched and dueled deliciously until they were both straining hard, their bodies duplicating the actions of their mouths.

With one arm, Jeff gripped her around her hips and urged her closer. Passion such as he'd never experienced before surged through him as he felt the softness of her woman's body envelop his throbbing heat. Wanting to taste more of her, he deepened the kiss and brought his other hand between them. He cupped her breast and knew a fierce satisfaction when he felt her nipple spring to life against the pad of his thumb.

He couldn't think, he couldn't do anything except give in to the life-giving urge to thrust against her softness, hoping she'd take him inside, hold him close and keep the fear at bay.

Hannah cried out. Her body was on fire, her breasts achy and swollen. Sensations exploded in the core of her body. She pulled her mouth away and gulped air.

Jeff eased his tight hold and released her. He sagged against the wall and stared at her. He was breathing raggedly, his eyes dilated in passion, and his skin was flushed.

"Stay with me tonight," he whispered hoarsely. He lifted his hand toward her.

Hannah knew he wasn't asking her to stay on as his houseguest. Slowly, unable to help herself, she placed her hand in his.

Chapter Nine

A tremor coursed through her body as their fingers met. Hoping it was excitement and not fear that had her reacting to his touch, Jeff smiled tenderly and drew her close against his side. He dropped a kiss on the top of her head, draped his arm around her shoulders and led her down the hallway to his bedroom.

The room was in semidarkness. The twinkling lights of the city and eerie glow of a full winter moon through the curtained window gave off enough light to see.

Vaguely aware that they'd stopped next to a king-size bed, Hannah nervously licked her lips and gazed around the shadowy bedroom. Jeff's arm dropped away from her shoulders and he stood quietly behind her, almost as if he were waiting for permission to touch her.

Slowly, Hannah turned. As she raised her gaze to meet his she inhaled sharply, stunned by the need reflected in the brilliant glow of his eyes. His mouth curved in a seductive smile, his chest rose and fell rapidly with each breath and the pulse point over his temple seemed to throb in time with the beating of her heart.

His desire was a palpable, living entity. It surged out of him like a bolt of invisible lightning and connected with the part of her she'd kept tightly sealed inside for so many years.

She exhaled slowly as a sense of peace descended upon her. This was right—whatever the cost, whatever price she had to pay. It no longer mattered. She couldn't walk away if her life depended on it.

Leaning forward, she stretched and lightly brushed her mouth against his, silently telling him to touch her.

That was what he was waiting for. With a low groan, Jeff pulled her tightly against him and slanted his mouth hungrily across hers.

His tongue sent a slow, sweet heat spreading through her whole body. She cried out softly and burrowed closer to his warmth. Her body ached to be held. Greedily, her mouth devoured his kisses as her hands clutched eagerly against the hard plane of his back.

Nothing mattered but this. All the fear and the pain and the worry were obliterated by the feel of his arms locked around her, by the scent of his clean, masculine flesh and the taste of his warm, sweet mouth.

Jeff suddenly pulled away and stepped back. Hannah gazed up at him in confusion. "What's wrong?"

He held her at arm's length, his fingers pressing hard into her shoulders. "I have to know," he said urgently, his voice harsh.

"Know what?" she whispered.

"If you'll regret this in the morning."

Regret it? Hannah knew he was giving her one last chance to walk away, one final opportunity to pretend they were nothing but friends. But she knew with utter certainty that she was past the point of no return. She didn't care that this was probably the most dangerous thing she'd ever do. She didn't care that she'd crossed some invisible line and that nothing would ever be the same again. She only knew she wanted him more than she'd ever wanted anything in her life.

"No," she said. "No regrets. Not tomorrow, not ever."

He searched her face for a moment. Relief surged through him and he smiled. In truth, Jeff didn't think he could have walked away if she'd answered differently. He needed her tonight.

He slid his hands to the top button of her blouse. His eyes bored into hers and his fingers shook as he opened the blouse and then slipped it off her shoulders.

Clad only in her lacy bra and slacks, she felt exposed. Shivering, she crossed her arms over her chest. But he was having none of that.

"Don't," he murmured, gently grabbing her wrists and shoving them behind her back. "Don't be shy with me. I've dreamed about seeing you like this," he said, holding her caged in his arms. "And my imagination wasn't nearly as good as I thought."

Her shyness evaporated when she saw the renewed flare of hunger on his face. Beneath the sheer white lace of her bra, her breasts swelled and her nipples hardened as she responded to the desire in his eyes.

Jeff unsnapped her bra and eased it off her shoulders. His hands went to the fastening of her slacks and she trembled as he pushed her clothes over her hips and down her legs.

His breath caught in his throat as he stared at her naked body. The ivory of her skin gleamed in the soft moonlight, her breasts were full and rounded and begging for his touch. He was awed. She was the most beautiful woman he'd ever seen and he ached for her.

Reaching behind her head, Jeff gently pulled out the pins holding her hair. Long auburn curls tumbled down and settled against her face and shoulders. She stood before him, her eyes wide and luminous, her mouth parted in an inviting smile, and he couldn't stand being separated from her an instant longer. He crushed her to him and covered her face with kisses.

Hannah sagged against him. She slipped her hands under his shirt and kneaded the muscles of his back. The low moans from his throat, the sensation of his body pressed hard against hers and the rigid bulge of his manhood swelling against her stomach made her blood race.

"I need you tonight," he muttered hoarsely, dragging his lips from hers. "God, do I need you."

Jeff tore himself away long enough to yank the spread back and then gently picked Hannah up and placed her between the cool sheets. He slipped out of his clothes quickly, kicking off his shoes and dumping his expensive suit into a heap on the floor.

Hannah watched as he undressed. His chest was wide and broad and covered with dark hair, his legs were long and heavily muscled, and his body was hard and throbbing with arousal.

Suddenly shy, she closed her eyes as he settled himself next to her. But Jeff wasn't going to let her retreat an inch. He pulled her to him and cupped her face between his palms.

"Look at me, Hannah," he murmured in a husky voice. "Don't be afraid of what's about to happen. I want you more than I've ever wanted a woman in my life. And I want you to want me just as much."

He kissed her, long and passionately. Desire surged through her, exquisite sensations erupted at every contact point where their flesh touched, her nerve endings quivered and her head was spinning. She couldn't breathe, couldn't think. She could only feel.

Jeff cupped her breast and gently rubbed his thumb back and forth across her nipple. She gasped in pleasure and tightened her arms around his neck.

He kissed her cheeks, her neck and shoulders. She trembled with each feather-light touch of his mouth to her skin. When he lowered his head and brought his mouth to her breast, she sighed and shifted restlessly against him, needing more. He took the taut peak between his lips, laved it lightly with his tongue and drew it into his mouth. She cried out as a powerful wave of desire tore through her and set up a low, pulsing ache deep in her belly.

His hands were stroking her body in long, slow motions. Then they began to tease the sensitive hollow between her thighs. She stiffened as his hand closed over her but he murmured softly in her ear, reassuring her. Gently, he stroked her softness until she relaxed and restlessly opened to his wondrous touch. She lifted her hips, arching against him as her body was rocked by wave after wave of sensual pleasure. She wanted, she needed, she ached for him.

Stretching her arms around him, she pulled him on top of her and kissed him passionately. His chest crushed her deliciously, their bodies were molded together and his hardness nestled in the hollow of her thighs.

Jeff could feel her along every centimeter of his flesh. His body was screaming for release and demanding that he bury himself deeply inside her and end this excruciating torment. Closing his eyes, he gritted his teeth against the powerful demands of his body and eased off her.

Hannah cried out as he suddenly pulled away. He shushed her with a quick kiss. "Just a sec," he said in a strained voice. "I've got to get something."

Leaning on one elbow, Jeff reached toward the nightstand by the bed and pulled open the drawer. Hannah heard the sound of a foil packet being opened and then he rolled away from her for a moment. She was inordinately touched by his care—God knows, she was too far gone to worry about precautions. But Jeff was a man she could trust.

That thought had just barely begun to take root in her mind when he moved to cover her again. And then she couldn't think at all.

He wedged himself between her legs and took her mouth in another slow, drugging kiss. Her thighs parted and she closed her eyes. Gently, he entered her.

Her body tensed at his intrusion. Fearing he was crushing her, Jeff pushed up on his arms. A fine sheen of perspiration glistened on his forehead and his muscles were shaking from the strain of holding back. The need to plunge completely inside her was almost overwhelming. "Are you all right?" he whispered, going perfectly still.

"Yes. Oh, yes." Hannah sighed deeply. "It's been a long time for me. Please...don't stop."

Slowly, he began to move. At first he was almost tentative. But as his desire mounted, as her body responded to his in the most fundamental way, he let go of his control.

He felt her quickening beneath him, heard her soft moans and sighs. He took her mouth in a hot, wet kiss and knew a fierce satisfaction as her tongue boldly rubbed against his, imitating the sensual movements of their bodies.

They spiraled upward as the tempo increased. Hannah matched him stroke for stroke. Jeff began to move hard and fast and for both of them the pressure built and built, climbing to an unbearable level of excitement.

Hannah cried out as the universe seemed to explode in her head. From what seemed far away, she heard Jeff's own low growl of pleasure. And then he went rigid for a split second before collapsing on top of her.

Their labored breathing sounded loud in the quiet aftermath of their heated lovemaking. After a few moments, Jeff rolled to the side and wrapped his arms around her.

His compulsion to touch her hadn't diminished. If anything, the pleasure and joy she'd given him made him want to hold her closer, more tightly. By imprinting himself upon her so forcibly, she'd be unable to deny what had really happened between them.

"My God, that was incredible," he said when he was able to find his voice. Propping his head on one elbow, he stared at her flushed face. She looked dazed. Her hair was tangled, her eyes half closed, and her lips were curved in a tiny, satisfied smile.

A great rush of tenderness filled him. Gently he smoothed the matted hair out of her eyes. "That was so good, Hannah. So right." He sighed in satisfaction. "Nothing's ever been that right before."

Hannah smiled sleepily and cuddled closer. She didn't want to think and she didn't want to talk. She only wanted to lie next to him and listen to the beating of his heart. But he seemed to be waiting for an answer. "It was wonderful for me, too," she told him honestly.

Jeff hesitated. One part of him wanted to force her to acknowledge what had just happened between them. To admit that what they'd shared wasn't just lust and sex. To admit there was a strong bond between them that had nothing to do with Kirsten or Irene or the transplant. But he couldn't push her. Not tonight. Not with the ordeal she had to face in the morning.

But he didn't want her turning over and going to sleep, either. There was still a question he had to ask. Jeff reached behind him and flicked on the brass lamp by the side of the bed. "What did you mean earlier?"

"Earlier?" Hannah echoed vaguely. She was disturbed by his serious tone. It meant he wanted to talk. Hoping he'd take a hint, she closed her eyes and snuggled deeper into the bedclothes.

"Hannah," he repeated impatiently, tugging her chin up so that she was forced to open her eyes. "Did you hear me?"

"Huh? Oh, yes." She yawned. "What are you talking about?"

"I want to know what you meant when you told me that your mother couldn't handle the idea of your getting close to your birth family."

Hannah sighed. She wished she hadn't said anything about Mary; it seemed so disloyal. But one part of her acknowledged he did have a right to know. He was, after all, stuck in the middle. And she felt so close to him now.

"My mother's a great person," she began hesitantly, fighting the feeling she was somehow betraying Mary. "She's sweet, kind, and one of the most unselfish people in the world. But she has this problem. She's terrified of birth families."

He raised his eyebrows. "That's a peculiar hang-up, isn't it?"

"Not really," Hannah stated. "Not when you understand her reasons." Unconsciously she began stroking the thick hair on his chest. "It all began when I was just a child. I had a younger sister named Hope. I was five when we adopted her but I can still remember how much we all loved her, especially my mother."

Hannah smiled as bittersweet memories flashed through her mind. "Anyway, after we'd had Hope for almost six months—long enough for all of us to get completely attached to her—the natural mother changed her mind and took her back. That's the law in this state. No adoption is final for six months. The birth mother can take the baby back anytime during that period."

Needing to concentrate on what she was saying, Jeff flattened Hannah's fingers against his chest. She didn't even notice. Her eyes were unfocused and far away, misted with painful memories.

"It hurt the whole family," she continued, "but it just about killed my mother. She became irrationally afraid of birth families. I remember when I was fourteen, I started asking her questions about my past. You know the sort of thing. Where had they adopted me from? Did they ever meet my natural parents, that kind of thing." Hannah slowly shook her head. "Mom started to cry, and she never cried. It frightened me so much, I shut right up and never mentioned the subject again."

"But that was years ago," Jeff said earnestly. "You're an adult now. Why is she still afraid? It's not like Irene can sue her for custody."

"You don't understand. Her fear isn't rational. She seems to have this deep-seated belief that if I have any contact with my birth family, I'll leave her."

Jeff smiled gently. "Has she told you that?"

"Not in so many words." Hannah felt a frisson of uneasiness race down her spine. She remembered her conversation with Mary the day before she'd come up here. Her mother had really taken the news surprisingly well. "But I know what she feels," she argued stubbornly. "She's my mother, for God's sake. She doesn't have to tell me."

"I don't doubt that," Jeff replied with a pacifying smile. "I'm only glad she didn't try to stop you from coming."

"She'd never do that. Despite her fear, she encouraged me to come up here and help. But I know what it's doing to her, how my being close to my sister must be affecting her."

Jeff frowned. "Does she know Irene is your natural mother."

Hannah swallowed and looked away. "No. I never mentioned that."

For a long moment, Jeff was silent. "I see," he finally said in a neutral voice. "Didn't you tell me your mother had gone to Mexico?"

"Well, y-yes," Hannah stammered. "But that doesn't have anything to do with it."

"Really?" he replied skeptically. "That doesn't sound like someone who's wringing her hands and worrying herself sick."

Hannah closed her eyes. He didn't understand. How could he? She felt his hand cup her chin.

"Hey," he said gently, "I didn't mean to upset you. Not tonight." Leaning down, he kissed her.

Hannah gave herself up to his embrace. She didn't want to talk anymore. She didn't want to think about her mother or her sister or tomorrow. Tonight she only wanted Jeff.

Excitement flared in his eyes as he pulled away and gave her a sexy grin. Turning, he flicked the lamp off and drew her close for another searing kiss.

A heavy white fog blanketed San Francisco the next morning. During the drive to the hospital, neither said more than ten words. Jeff concentrated on the traffic and Hannah was too anxious about the extraction procedure to make casual conversation.

By the time they reached the glass doors of the hospital lobby, Hannah was as nervous as a skittish cat and her stomach was growling.

"You must be hungry," Jeff muttered absently, holding the door open for her. They hadn't had breakfast. Hannah wasn't allowed to eat or drink because she was having a general anesthetic.

"I'd kill for a cup of coffee," she replied, glancing around the deserted lobby.

Jeff didn't appear to hear her. He led the way to the elevators and then abruptly stopped and turned to face her.

"I need to tell you something before you go up," he said earnestly.

His tone bothered her. Her fingers tightened on the handle of the overnight case she carried. "What is it?" she asked apprehensively. "Is something wrong?"

Jeff stared at her somberly. "Whatever happens," he said softly, "whatever the outcome of all this, I want you to know I'll always be grateful."

Hannah's heart began to thud.

"Last night," he continued in a low, urgent voice, "you saved me. The way you made love with me, the way you gave yourself so completely, it was exactly what I needed. You kept the fear away and helped me forget what we were facing today. Hannah, I'll never forget it."

He paused and took a deep breath, hoping he was making her understand what their lovemaking had meant to him. "So, no matter what happens with the transplant, I want you to know I'll be grateful to you for the rest of my life."

Her stomach turned over. She felt sick. This was a nightmare come to life. Last night she'd convinced herself that he felt something meaningful for her and that his lovemaking had been an expression of the feeling.

But she'd been wrong. She'd been a complete fool. He was *grateful*.

Tears clogged her throat but she swallowed hard and fought them back. Of all the things he could have said to her, this was the worst. She smiled tightly as a wave of nausea hit her.

Idiot! she screamed silently to herself. Last night had only been a temporary diversion for him. Like taking an aspirin for a headache. She'd been merely a pleasant way of helping him forget his troubles. Bitterness welled up in her throat and almost choked her.

Blindly, she reached over and jabbed the elevator button, praying that at this time in the morning it would come quickly so she could escape.

It's my own fault, she thought wretchedly, turning away so she wouldn't have to look at him. I knew it would be like this. I knew it, I knew it...

"Hannah?" he asked worriedly when she remained silent. "Is everything all right? Did I say something wrong?" He tugged on her arm, forcing her to face him.

Hannah kept her face completely blank. She'd just made the mistake of her life, but she refused to let him see what his damned gratitude was doing to her.

"Nothing's wrong," she said with a brittle smile. "I just want this over with. I'm glad I was able to help last night."

Jeff looked hurt. "I didn't mean it like that," he said stonily. "You make it sound like you dropped in to bring me a casserole. I wasn't using you last night. What happened between us is separate from this. It's personal."

"No, it's not," she countered tightly. "You just said so yourself. Last night we both needed to forget. Like it or not, this—" she gestured quickly around the hospital "—is all bound up with what happened."

He was seized by a quiet panic. Something was wrong. The elevator came, but before he could make her tell him what was bothering her, what he'd said wrong, she stepped inside and punched the floor button.

Jeff didn't know what to say. She was right and she was wrong, and he had the awful feeling his attempt to tell her what she meant to him had backfired. "We'll talk about this later," he yelled as the door shut in his face.

Hannah let her mind go blank. When she got off on the oncology floor, she wasn't nervous about the extraction procedure anymore. She was numb.

She didn't want to think. Hannah gave herself completely into the hands of the medical staff and things started happening fast. Within seconds, a nurse had whisked her off to her room. She changed into a hospital gown and then was helped onto a gurney.

As she waited for the orderly to wheel her down to the operating room, Hannah stared at the overhead lights.

Deliberately, she refused to think about Jeff, or about Kirsten or her mother. Instead, she forced herself to go over every detail of the bone-marrow extraction. Gruesome as it was, it was the least painful thing she could call to mind.

She would be put to sleep. Then four to eight small incisions would be made in her pelvic region and twenty to thirty extractions would be done through the incisions. They would take between 500 and 800 milliliters of fluid, containing three to five percent of her total bone marrow.

How much of her heart had she given last night?

The fluid would then go through a process called "harvesting," to remove blood and bone-fragments before being injected into Kirsten.

It was simple. There was nothing to worry about. But the last thought that drifted through Hannah's mind as she stared up into the masked face of the anesthesiologist was that she wished Jeff had kissed her goodbye.

When she woke up, she was groggy and stiff.

The piercing light in the recovery room hurt her eyes, so Hannah squeezed her lids closed. Her mouth was parched. She heard a soft moan and was startled to realize it came from her throat. "I'm thirsty," she managed to croak.

"You can't have anything to drink until we know you're fully conscious," answered a crisp voice.

Hannah cringed and opened her eyes. A nurse was smiling down at her. In her hand she held a small cup. "I know you're thirsty. You can drink this in a minute. But we've got to make sure you've come out of the anesthetic first."

"What time is it?" Her voice sounded slurred. "Where am I?"

"It's just past noon," the nurse replied cheerfully. "And you're in Recovery. We'll take you back to your room in a few minutes."

Hannah swallowed painfully. There was a bitter taste in her mouth. "How did the extraction go?"

The nurse ignored that question. "Don't try to move yet," she instructed. "The doctor will be by to talk to you soon."

As promised, as soon as the nurse was sure she could swallow without choking to death, she was given a drink of water. The doctor popped his head into Recovery long enough to tell Hannah things had gone fine during the extraction. Then she was moved to her room.

She was staying overnight to make sure there was no excessive blood loss from the procedure. Hannah thought they were being unduly cautious, even going so far as having taken a unit of her own blood before doing the procedure and keeping it on hand, just in case.

She slept on and off for the rest of the day. She remembered waking up once and seeing Jeff standing over her. But she'd fallen back to sleep before she could say anything.

When she finally awoke to full consciousness, it was pitch black outside. She was in a private room and no one had bothered to draw the blinds. In the hallway, she could hear the muffled voices and footsteps of the staff.

She reached over and found the mechanism that moved the bed. Raising herself to a sitting position, Hannah poured herself a glass of water from the jug on the nightstand. She sipped the water and stared out into the night. The moon was gone. She smiled bitterly.

It was finished. Everything was over. San Francisco, the extraction, Jeff. A hysterical laugh welled up in her throat but she gamely fought it down. Hannah took a deep breath and clenched her hands into fists.

There was no reason to stay. Not anymore.

Kirsten's life was in the hands of God and the doctors.

And Jeff was grateful.

By the time the first rays of the sun broke through the darkness, she'd made up her mind. Kirsten wasn't due for the infusion of her bone marrow for a couple of days and Hannah had originally thought she'd wait until that was over before going home. But now that was impossible.

She had to leave.

Dr. Trevisi came by early that morning. He looked surprised that Hannah insisted on being released immediately, but he left to do as she asked.

Hannah panicked when the door opened again, thinking it was Jeff coming to see her. She knew she couldn't face him. Not yet. Maybe not ever. But it was only a nurse with a breakfast tray.

Hungry as she was, she ignored the food and slipped into her clothes. Her hips hurt and she was frustrated by her slow, clumsy movements. But the pain in her body was not nearly as acute as the pain in her heart.

She stopped by the business office to sign some papers on her way out. She waited until after nine, when she knew Jeff would already be upstairs for his morning visit with Kirsten before she went down to the lobby to call a cab.

Letting herself into his apartment, she paused by the door and listened, wanting to be doubly sure that Jeff wasn't there. But she heard nothing.

Hannah limped into her bedroom. Her suitcase was sitting on her bed, still open from her frenzied packing two nights ago. If it were possible, she'd have laughed. But she was afraid to give in to feeling anything. It hurt too much.

It took her less than ten minutes to pack. She winced as she picked up her suitcase and overnight bag. Her hip had stiffened even further and her entire pelvic region throbbed painfully. The analgesics she'd been given at the hospital were wearing off. Moving slowly, Hannah made her way into the hallway. When she stopped to catch her breath, she found herself staring into Jeff's bedroom.

Tears welled in her eyes and she hastily brushed them away. Taking a deep, steadying breath she dropped her suitcases and opened her purse. Snatching out the vial of pills they'd given her, she went into the bathroom for a glass of water.

The fragrance of his scent slammed into her with the impact of a fist. He'd left the top of his after-shave off. Hannah's throat worked convulsively to keep from crying. She decided to wait until she reached the airport to take the pills.

Hannah picked up her bags. From the den, the phone rang. She froze. She knew it was Jeff.

It rang ten times and then went silent. She dropped her bags and hobbled into the den, snatched the receiver up and frantically dialed information for the number of the taxi company before he could call back. Keeping an eye on the telephone, she grabbed a piece of paper from his desk and hastily scribbled Jeff a note. She owed him that much.

She knew he'd call back. By now he must realize she'd checked out. He was a nice man; of course he'd be concerned. But then Kevin had been a nice man, too—so nice that it took her months to realize he didn't love her; he'd only been grateful. Just as Jeff was.

Chapter Ten

Jeff was half out of his mind with worry; Hannah hadn't answered the phone all day. He'd tried repeatedly to reach her but the fates were working against him. One crisis after another had chained him to his office till after five, and then he'd been stuck in traffic for half an hour on the Bay Bridge.

Jeff cursed everything on wheels as he unlocked the door of his apartment. "Hannah!" he yelled, stepping inside and then stopping abruptly. The rooms were dark and ominously silent. Flicking on the light switch, he shouted again. "Hannah, where are you? Answer me, damn it!"

Silence.

Jeff swept the living room with one quick glance and strode toward her bedroom. He stopped and his heart began to pound against his ribs as he saw her house keys on top of the coffee table. There was a folded sheet of notepaper next to them.

A terrible sense of impending disaster had dogged him since he'd discovered Hannah had left the hospital without a word. But he'd convinced himself she'd checked out because she didn't particularly like hospitals. That was the only way he'd made it through the day.

For what seemed an eternity, he stared down at the note. Finally he gathered his courage and picked it up.

Dear Jeff,
I decided it was time to go home. I hope everything goes well for Kirsten. I'll call you in a few weeks to check on her progress. Thank you for your wonderful hospitality.

Sincerely, Hannah

He couldn't believe it. Jeff blinked and read it again—several times. But the words didn't change. She'd left. Vanished. Flown the coop and disappeared out of his life with a polite little note thanking him for his hospitality.

He stared dazedly around the living room. The whole place echoed with emptiness, as if she'd stolen all his joy and warmth and taken it with her when she walked out the door.

The anxiety that had simmered quietly within him since he'd found her gone from the hospital this morning boiled over into anger. Her rejection slashed at him like a knife. Rage and pain flooded his whole system.

Jeff crumpled the note into a tight ball and smashed it against the floor. He closed his eyes. In the distance he could hear the mournful sound of a foghorn. For several minutes he just stood there, getting his anger under control. Then he reached for the telephone and dialed her number.

She answered on the second ring. "Hello."

"Hannah, it's Jeff." He heard her clear her throat. "What the hell's going on?"

"Nothing's going on," she replied coolly. "It was just time to leave. That's all. Is everything all right with Kirsten?"

"Kirsten's fine," he snapped. Jeff gritted his teeth and clamped down the lid on his temper. "I'm the one with the problem."

Hannah didn't answer him for several moments. Then he heard her sigh softly.

"I'm sorry," she murmured. "But I had to leave." She paused. "I thought it would be best to clear out before things got any more complicated. We made a terrible mistake."

"Mistake?" Jeff repeated incredulously. "What are you talking about? That's ridiculous. How can you call our making love a mistake? For God's sake, that was the most wonderful night of my life!"

"You only think that because of the circumstances," she said hastily. Hannah refused to let him delude himself anymore. One day the illusion would end and reality would hit him with the shock of an eight-point earthquake. Sooner or later, he'd realize precisely what had brought them together. And it had nothing to do with love.

"Don't you understand?" she blurted out. "What happened between us wasn't *real*."

"It felt damned real to me," he bit out caustically. "It felt damned good, too. Too good to walk away from."

She smiled bitterly. He was as good as telling her she was right. But lust was no substitute for love. "You're deliberately misunderstanding me. I'm not talking about the physical part of it. I'm talking about our emotions, our reasons for coming together."

"I'm talking about emotions, too, Hannah," he stated flatly. "And the reason it was so good is because of the way we feel about each other."

Hannah couldn't afford to believe him. "No. You made love to me because you needed a warm body. Someone to keep the fear away, someone to help you get through the night. We were playing a game," she said desperately. "We were using each other because we didn't want to have to think about what was going to happen the next morning."

"That's ridiculous," he snapped.

"No, it's not," she insisted. "You're grateful to me. You're physically attracted to me. But you don't really want *me*—not for any kind of relationship. I know you think you do, but you're wrong."

"How do you know?" he demanded, his hand tightening on the receiver. "What makes you such an expert on my feelings? Or is it *your* emotions we're talking about here?"

Hannah ignored that last accusation. She bit her lip, hard. "I've been in situations like this before," she answered slowly, choosing her words with care. "I know what I'm talking about. Believe me, Jeff, I wish with all my heart that things were different. But I learned a long time ago to face reality."

"Then face this reality," he insisted. "I care about you and I need you. I don't know what's happened to you in the past and I don't know why you keep saying you've been in this situation before. All I know is we have something special going and I don't want to lose it."

Hannah couldn't answer. She could only focus on one thing. He'd said he "needed" her. Bitterness clutched at her heart and made it difficult to breathe. Oh, he needed her, all right, she thought dismally— but not as a woman, not as someone he wanted to keep in his life permanently.

Jeff wanted an anchor. A lifeline. A warm body to help him cope with the daily pain of watching his sister struggle to stay alive. He wanted her physically and he was grateful to her, but that was all it was. And one day, he'd realize that himself.

Her silence scared him. "Hannah, answer me."

What could she say? He wasn't capable of seeing the truth about their relationship. "You're not being fair...."

"Life isn't fair," he interrupted, hitting her hard and not caring that he wasn't playing by the rules. "Didn't our night together mean anything at all?"

"Of course, it did."

"Then come back. For God's sake, don't turn your back on what we shared, what we could have together."

"But that's just it!" she cried. "I know what we could have together and it isn't what you think. It isn't anything that'll last."

"You can't know that!" he yelled, panicking at the finality in her tone. He broke off and brought himself back under control. "There's something wonderful between us, something good, something worth fighting to hang on to," he said urgently. "You can't just walk away from it. Come on, Hannah. If I mean anything at all to you, you'll give us a chance."

Kevin Webster's painful rejection flashed through her mind. But instead of cringing from the memory, Hannah snatched at it and held on to it for dear life. She straightened her spine. When she spoke, her voice was flat and utterly implacable. "I can't."

Hope drained out of him. Jeff stared blindly into the distance. "So that's it, then? This is goodbye?"

"I'm sorry," she replied stiffly. "But it has to be this way."

He heard the soft click on the end of the line.

Carefully Jeff put the phone down and went to the liquor cabinet in the corner. He poured himself a double Scotch and sank down onto the couch.

How could she do it? he wondered angrily, taking a gulp from the glass. How could she walk away from what they'd shared together? From what they felt for each other?

But what did Hannah feel for him? The faint question from the back of his mind sent a shaft of fear rippling down his spine, so he brushed it aside.

Hannah hadn't made sense at all. Her leaving didn't make sense. He shook his head. Nothing made sense. What the hell had she been talking about? Of course, it was real between them.

Then how could she turn her back and walk away from what they had, from what they'd shared? A wave of bitterness churned in his stomach and mixed with the Scotch.

He'd been living on hope for the past week. One by one, Hannah's defenses had crumbled and she'd let him get close. He'd thought it was because she was starting to trust him, starting to understand that their relationship was special.

Jeff laughed harshly. It was special, all right, he decided cynically; so damned special she took off the first chance she got.

He took another long sip. The fiery liquid burned his throat and temporarily obliterated the pain raging through him.

He'd spent the day fighting the feeling that something was terribly wrong. Maybe his subconscious had been trying to tell him something. Maybe she didn't give a damn about him.

He shifted uncomfortably against the leather cushions as her words echoed in his mind. "We were playing a game. We were using each other because we didn't want to face what was going to happen the next morning." Jeff closed his eyes, and Hannah's face as she'd gotten on the elevator yesterday swam before him. He remembered those words, too. "I'm glad I was able to help."

That had hurt. But he'd excused her because they were both so uptight about Kirsten that neither of them was thinking straight.

What did *Hannah feel for him?* He couldn't ignore the question anymore. A tormenting suspicion began to harden into certainty. Jeff's fingers tightened around the glass.

Her reasons didn't matter. She just didn't want him. He wondered why she'd let him make love to her and then sucked in his breath as the truth hit him: she had made love to him because she felt sorry for him and she wanted to help him forget for a few hours.

A dull ache spread through his whole body. He gulped in another ragged breath. The one thing he couldn't take from Hannah was pity.

Jeff swallowed the last of the Scotch and laughed bitterly. He knew exactly what Hannah felt for him now: nothing. Absolutely nothing, because pity didn't count.

Slowly he raised his arm and hurled the empty glass against the wall.

The next three weeks passed in a dull, gray haze for Hannah. It wasn't so bad when she was at work. There was plenty to do. No one had covered her desk while she was gone. But the nights were an agony to endure.

Sleep evaded her. Every time she closed her eyes she was taunted by memories. Her head would hit the pillow and images of Jeff would torment her relentlessly for hours. She could see his face, alive and animated as they debated the latest political scandal. She remembered the taste of his lips as he kissed her tenderly; and sometimes she could even feel his hands sliding sensually over her body and igniting a flame of hot desire so real she ached from wanting him.

And the days were no better. No matter how hard she tried, she couldn't get the man out of her head. Even surrounded by people, she was lonely. Her appetite dwindled to nothing and for the first time in her life she had to use concealer under her eyes to hide the dark circles.

One of her male colleagues used the same aftershave Jeff did. Hannah had accidentally bumped into the man in the hall and the familiar scent hit her so unexpectedly, tears had sprung to her eyes. Hurriedly excusing herself, she'd practically run back to her office.

Every time the phone rang, her heart leaped into her throat. But it was never Jeff. And she couldn't bring herself to call him, though she missed him so much it was like walking around with an open wound.

Mary returned from Mexico, tanned and bubbling with enthusiasm over her experiences at the orphanage. Hannah expected the third degree about San Francisco, but all her mother asked was how things had gone and would Kirsten Kenyon have a chance now.

A few days after Mary's return, Hannah got lassoed into going to a church potluck and slide show about the orphanage.

Holding a bucket of fried chicken to her chest, Hannah reluctantly descended the steps into the church hall and glanced around for her mother. She spotted Mary huddled with Pastor McMahon over a stack of slides. She stopped on the bottom step, struck by the way the two of them were so absorbed in each other. Cocking her head to one side, she watched them.

Mary's face practically glowed. She was holding a slide up to the light and talking excitedly to John, who stood gazing back at her like a love-struck teenager.

They're a cute couple, Hannah thought, jolted by a sudden pleasure at seeing her mother so happy. She didn't want to intrude, so she quickly made her way to the nearest empty table and sat down.

Mary turned and saw her. She tossed the slide onto the table and waved. "Hi, sweetie!" she called, coming toward her with outstretched arms. "I'm so glad you decided to come," she continued breathlessly, giving Hannah a hug. She stepped back and examined her daughter from head to foot. "Aren't you feeling well?" Her brow wrinkled. "My goodness, you're pale. And you've lost weight, too."

"I'm fine," Hannah fibbed quickly. "I've just been putting in a lot of hours at the community center. But I've caught up now, so I can ease off some."

"Well, I'm glad you came tonight. You've practically become a hermit!"

"Things will be better now," Hannah replied cheerfully. It took every ounce of acting ability she possessed to make her voice sound natural. "Of course, I came. I wouldn't miss seeing the slides of your trip for anything."

Mary grinned. "Good. Maybe next year you'll consider going down. The experience is unbelievable."

Someone called for Mary from the kitchen, so she hustled Hannah to the table where she and the pastor were sitting and turned to go. She hesitated a moment and asked, "Can you have dinner with John and me tomorrow night?"

"Tomorrow night?" Hannah didn't really want to go out with her mother. The strain of pretending everything was normal was already beginning to wear on her. But she didn't want Mary guessing there was something wrong. "Sure," she replied.

By the time the lights were dimmed and the first picture flashed on the screen, Hannah's face hurt from the effort of smiling.

One of the teenage girls did the narration and surprisingly enough, Hannah soon found herself totally absorbed.

The slides were dramatic and heartbreakingly beautiful. There was scene after scene of bright-eyed children wearing raggedy, mismatched clothes but grinning happily into the camera, despite the poverty obvious in the background.

Pastor McMahon and Mary were prominent in many of the shots. Hannah stole a quick glance at her mother after one particularly poignant scene. The room was darkened but there was still enough light to see the pastor's hand resting on her mother's arm.

Startled, Hannah quickly looked away. But it made her think. Her mother had been awfully busy since coming back from Mexico. Every time Hannah had phoned her, Mary was either on her way out somewhere with John or just leaving for the church to help with something or other. If Hannah's brain had been functioning properly, she'd have realized sooner what was happening.

Her mother was behaving like a woman in love.

The next night, her suspicions were confirmed.

John took them to an elegant seafood restaurant in Solana Beach on old Highway 101. The pastor startled Hannah when he insisted on ordering a bottle of champagne.

As soon as the waiter poured the sparkling liquid, John shyly cleared his throat and raised his glass. "Hannah," he began hesitantly, "I've asked your mother to do me the honor of becoming my wife."

Taken aback, Hannah stared at them.

John frowned worriedly. "You don't have any objections, do you, my dear?"

"Oh, my goodness, no!" she answered, breaking into a delighted laugh. "Of course not. I don't know why I'm so surprised. Anyone with half a brain could see how wonderful you two are together."

She reached over and hugged her mother. "Oh, Mom, I'm so happy for you. And for you, too," she said, turning in her chair and leaning to kiss John on the cheek. "Welcome to the family."

"Thank you, dear," Mary replied with a chuckle. "We haven't set a date yet, but it'll be soon." She grinned impishly at her fiancé. "Neither of us is getting any younger."

The next morning, Hannah's mood was considerably lighter. Her mother's happiness had momentarily obscured her own misery—so much so that she was actually humming as she made her way to the tiny kitchen at the back of the community center for a cup of coffee. The humming turned into a groan when she saw the stack of manila files sitting next to her mug. A note with her name on it was lying on top.

Hannah sighed, poured herself a cup of coffee, and picked up the folders. She was trying to decipher Beverly's handwriting when she bumped into a chair hard enough to slosh coffee all over her hand and send the files flying in all directions.

Darn! she muttered to herself, shaking coffee off her hand and glaring at the chair. What idiot left that here? She looked suspiciously at the row of open doors lining the hall.

Hannah bent down, set her cup on the floor and gathered up the scattered files. From inside the nearest office, she could hear the soft voice of Kim Weiner, one of the center's social workers.

"Leah, I know this is a hard decision for you. But it has to be your decision. No one else's. It's going to affect both you and the baby for the rest of your life."

Hannah went perfectly still. There was a strangled sob and a tearful voice said, "But that's just it. I don't know what to do. I don't know what's best. I need someone to tell me what to do."

"Leah, I can't do that," Kim continued gently. "This is *your* life we're talking about. You're the one who'll have to live with the consequences. All I can do is help you sort out your feelings. Whether or not you give the baby up for adoption has to be your choice. I can't tell you what to do. This has to be your decision."

Hannah had heard enough. Hastily she gathered up the rest of the files and hurried to her office. Her hands were shaking as she dumped the files on her desk. She knew what she'd overheard and it had shaken her to the core.

Leah Hofstadter was a pregnant teenager who'd come to the center for counseling. The girl was grappling with whether or not to give her baby up for adoption. She was seventeen and a high-school dropout with few prospects for the future. But Hannah had heard the torment in that voice; the plea for someone else to make this most painful decision for her.

Sighing, Hannah sat down and stared vacantly at the stack of files. A heavy depression settled on her. She began to wonder if Irene had gone through the kind of torment that Leah Hofstadter was facing. Had her birth mother once sat in a dingy little office and pleaded with someone to tell her what to do? Had she, too, been ripped apart by an agonizing decision that might have the power to haunt her the rest of her life?

The thought disturbed her. Hannah mentally shook herself and picked up the first folder on the pile. She considered herself a professional; she shouldn't be reacting this way. Life was full of painful choices. Getting emotional about Leah and her unborn child wouldn't do either of them any good.

But, try as she might, she couldn't concentrate on the work in front of her. Leah's pathetic voice kept intruding into her mind and she found herself hoping that the girl would make the right decision.

Lost in her thoughts, she stared blindly at the calendar on her desk. Her eyes focused on the bright-red *X* she'd drawn in the middle of the page. With a start she realized what the huge crimson reminder meant.

It had been over three weeks since the extraction. The infusion of her marrow into Kirsten's body, a procedure called the "rescue" had taken place a couple of days after she left. Hannah remembered the doctor telling her the engraftment process usually occurred between fourteen and thirty days after the transplant.

Suddenly desperate to know if there was any news, she stared at the phone. She'd call Jeff. Hannah reached for the phone and then hesitated, took a deep breath and told herself not to be ridiculous. He might have thought the way she'd left was a bit rude, but if he'd cared about her at all he'd have contacted her.

The thought brought a fresh stab of pain, and she clenched her hands into fists. She smiled cynically. Obviously Jeff had come to the same conclusions that she had about their relationship. All that specialness he'd gone on about was nothing more than passion and gratitude. She'd been right, all along. He didn't care. But being right brought her little joy.

Her fingers trembled as she dialed the number of Kenyon International.

* * *

"Call on line two, Jeff." His secretary's cheerful voice grated on his nerves.

"Thanks, Brenda," he muttered into the intercom. Jeff sighed heavily, picked up the receiver and punched the blinking button. "Jeff Kenyon."

"Jeff, it's Hannah."

Her voice sent a bittersweet rush of pleasure surging through him. A seed of hope blossomed deep inside him. Maybe she was calling for another chance. Maybe she'd missed him as much as he'd missed her.

At his silence, she swallowed painfully. "Jeff?"

"I'm here," he said. His grip tightened around the receiver. "I was afraid I'd never hear from you again."

"I'm calling to see how Kirsten's doing," she blurted out. "The doctor said the grafting process might have started by now. It's been over three weeks."

Jeff smiled bitterly. Hannah wasn't calling because she'd missed him. She was calling to check up on Kirsten. The seed of hope withered to nothing. "So far," he replied coolly, "things are going fine. But we'll know more in the next couple of weeks. The doctors are cautiously optimistic."

"Oh. Well, I'm glad she seems to be doing all right. Can I call you in a couple of weeks to see how things are?"

God, he couldn't take that. He couldn't take hearing her voice and knowing she didn't give a damn about him; knowing she didn't care.

"You can call Dr. Trevisi. We've authorized him to release information about Kirsten's condition to you. I thought I told you that before you left."

"You did," Hannah replied, swallowing hard. "I just forgot. I'll call him the next time."

"Was there anything else?" Jeff asked coldly.

"No, no. Nothing else. Well, I hope things continue going well." There was a long pause and then she said, "Goodbye."

Jeff sat like a statue, holding the receiver to his ear. Finally when he heard the dial tone, he carefully set it down.

He'd been abrupt with her, deliberately so. But the very sound of her voice had been like a fist slamming into his gut.

She'd gone, left him, walked away without a backward glance, and it had hurt like hell. It still hurt. But lately, mostly because of Irene's gentle probing, he'd tried looking at the whole situation from Hannah's point of view.

Then, why had he been so damned rude to her on the phone?

Because he was hurting, that's why.

An image of Hannah flashed into his mind. Beautiful, pale, disheveled from their lovemaking and looking up at him with those wary, big brown eyes of hers. He sat back and flattened his hands on the desk. He tried to think calmly.

The call had been a first step—not a particularly big step, but a first step nonetheless. Hannah could have called Dr. Trevisi about Kirsten. He didn't believe for a minute that she'd forgotten that.

But she'd called him.

And he'd blown it.

He missed her so much. Since she'd left, there had been a huge, gaping hole in his life. He missed their lively conversations and her impish grin when she'd scored a particularly good point for her side. He missed sharing a glass of wine in front of the fire with her. Hell, he even missed her things cluttering up his bathroom. Jeff raked a hand through his hair as he thought of something else he missed—making love to her. He must have relived that night a thousand times in his mind.

He slammed his fist down on his desk and stared straight ahead for a few moments. Then, his decision made, he jabbed the button on the intercom. "Brenda, cancel my appointments for the rest of the day," he ordered. "I'm leaving."

Hannah deliberately worked late. Mary was off to a women's retreat for the weekend and she wasn't up to facing her empty apartment. Jeff's coolness on the phone had plunged her into despair.

So she buried herself in work. By seven-thirty, she was exhausted enough to risk going home.

Hannah parked her car and killed the lights. She pulled her jacket tighter against the cool wind and hurried across the parking lot.

Her head was bent as she dug her keys out of her purse when a familiar voice froze her in her tracks.

"Hello, Hannah." Jeff slowly stepped out of the shadows.

Chapter Eleven

Hannah stared at Jeff. She stood paralyzed, not with fear, but with an emotion just as dangerous. She forgot everything as a surge of fierce joy made her so giddy, her knees started to shake.

Jeff walked toward her slowly, stopping a few feet away in a pool of light thrown by the overhead street-lamp. He wore jeans and his black corduroy jacket, its collar turned up against the bitter wind. Uncertain of his welcome after the way he'd spoken to her on the phone, he simply waited.

She couldn't know that he'd broken every speed limit between here and San Francisco. That he was desperate to see her again, to make things right between them. She couldn't know he'd been so scared of losing her that when he'd arrived and found her apartment dark and empty, he'd panicked.

"Jeff," she said huskily, her pleasure at seeing him evident in her voice. "Is it really you? Are you really here?"

Jeff exhaled the breath he'd been holding. "I came to apologize," he said softly.

"Apologize?" she echoed, taken aback. "What on earth for? I'm the one who should be sorry."

"Being so rude on the phone," he answered quickly. "My only excuse is that I was hurt." He shrugged. "Like a lot of people, I lash out in stupid ways when I'm hurt."

Hannah's brown eyes grew as big as saucers. Her pulse leaped into double time. She couldn't believe what she was hearing. "It's all right," she murmured. "You had every right to be angry. I shouldn't have left the way I did."

"I didn't say I was angry, Hannah," he corrected gently, determined to make her understand. "I said I was hurt."

A cold gust of wind slammed into them and he looked pointedly at her door. "May I come in?"

"Oh, yes, of course." Hannah led the way into her apartment. She slipped off her coat and tossed it along with her purse onto the couch. "You must be hungry. Would you like a sandwich?"

"No," he answered. Jeff leaned back against the door and stared at her. She wore a form-fitting brown knit dress with a draped cowl neck. The slinky garment clung to her delicate curves like a second skin. Her hair was pinned up, revealing the elegant lines of her neck and throat. Small gold hoop earrings dangled from her ears. She was twisting her hands together in front of her as she watched him from across the small space separating them. She looked flustered. Nervous. Beautiful.

He had to handle this carefully. He was determined to have a whole relationship with her. The past three weeks without her had convinced him of one thing: he'd do anything to get Hannah back into his life.

"Jeff," she asked hesitantly as he continued to stare at her, "do you want some coffee?"

He shoved away from the door and walked toward her. Stopping inches away from her, he cupped her face between his hands and stared at her intently.

"Right now, the only thing I'm thirsty for is you. But I have to know—" his gaze bored into hers "—do you care for me at all? Do I mean anything to you?"

The scent of her perfume filled his lungs. He could feel the warm heat of her body brushing seductively against him. More than anything, he wanted to crush her to him and kiss her senseless. But he held himself rigidly in check. He had to know how she felt about him; had to know if his instincts about them were right, or if he was only chasing an idiot's dream.

Hannah was thrown completely off balance. Her mouth opened and then closed again. She couldn't lie; she couldn't do anything against the hard demand in his brilliant gaze except tell him the truth. "Yes," she whispered hoarsely. "I care about you."

"As your lover? Or your half sister's brother?" His hands tightened around her face.

Hannah stared at him helplessly. One look at his expression told her he was going to be relentless. His gaze was powerful and compelling and utterly honest. She felt as though she were looking into his soul, and what she saw forced the truth to her lips: "As a lover."

The instant she said the words, she felt curiously liberated. She *did* want Jeff as a lover, she wanted him whatever way she could have him. Since the minute she'd walked out of his apartment, she'd felt isolated and empty. Without him, she'd been living a hellish nightmare of loneliness and misery. The price she might have to pay no longer mattered. Nothing mattered except being with him.

Jeff sighed with relief and pulled her close. "Ah, Hannah," he muttered hoarsely, "that was the right answer."

Her cheek rested against his chest. She loved the feel of his arms crushing her, loved the scent of his warm, masculine heat and the mesmerizing sound of his heart beating against her ear. She suddenly didn't care if he wanted her because of gratitude, or lust, or simply because she was available.

"I've missed you so much," she whispered raggedly.

He laughed and she could feel the vibrations rumbling through his chest. "Not half as much as I've missed you." Sobering, he pulled away and held her at arm's length. When she raised her eyes to meet his, there wasn't a hint of amusement in his face. He looked serious.

"Why did you leave?" he asked, his voice low and urgent. Jeff had to know what had sent her fleeing from his apartment. "Did I do something wrong? Did I say something that upset you?"

Hannah couldn't answer him. She lowered her gaze and stared at the floor.

He gave her a gentle shake. "You've got to tell me," he persisted. "It's been driving me crazy. For God's sake, one minute we're lovers and the next minute you're gone. I've got to know why!''

She bit her lower lip. What could she say? The truth would sound so pathetic. How could she tell him she'd been running from his gratitude, from those kind but heartbreaking words he'd said to her that morning in the hospital?

"Hannah—" his voice was soft, but insistent "—tell me."

"It was what you said that morning before the extraction," she blurted miserably. "You were so damned grateful. You didn't say you felt anything else." She raised her eyes to meet his. "I'm so scared this isn't real, that it's nothing more than gratitude on your part. And I want you so much, I can't think straight."

It took a moment for her meaning to sink in. Then Jeff shook his head, his expression thoughtful. "Of course I was grateful," he explained, choosing his words with care. "Any decent person would appreciate what you did for us. But if you think that's the only thing I feel for you, you're out of your mind. I care about you and I want you. The past three weeks have been the most miserable of my life."

"Are you sure?" she asked gravely.

Tenderness washed over him as he looked down into her worried brown eyes. "As soon as I hung up this morning," he confessed softly, "I knew I had to see you. I told my secretary to cancel my appointments, threw some clothes into a bag and drove like a kamikaze pilot to get down here on the off chance that you'd been as miserable as I was. Does that sound like a man motivated by gratitude?"

"No." Hannah blinked rapidly against the sudden wetness in her eyes. But, reassuring as his words were, she knew she couldn't afford to believe them. Yet it didn't seem to matter anymore. She'd grab what she could of him now and steel herself against the inevitable pain of losing him when the time came—when he finally realized that the only real bonds between them were gratitude and passion. It would happen; but maybe, if she were very, very lucky, it wouldn't happen for a long time.

"Then, come away with me for the weekend."

"Where?" Hannah was ready to follow him anywhere.

He gave her a slow, sexy grin. "Neutral territory." She looked so surprised he laughed aloud. "I want to take you someplace where we can concentrate on each other." He glanced around her apartment, his gaze stopping at the photograph of her parents. "We need to talk and make love and get close again. I want us to be away from everything but each other."

What he really meant was that they needed time without any reminders of their families. Jeff was convinced that half their problem was the crazy circumstances that had brought them together.

"Neutral territory." Hannah repeated the words slowly as a radiant smile spread across her face. "Yes. I think that's exactly what we need," she agreed. Stepping away, she headed for her bedroom. "I can be ready in ten minutes. I just need to change and throw a few things into a bag."

"Fine. I'll make us a reservation at a hotel I know up the coast." He glanced at his watch. "We can be there by midnight. But Hannah—" his voice stopped her as she reached the hall and she turned "—do me a favor. Don't change that dress—I like it."

At precisely eleven fifty-five that evening, Hannah followed Jeff into a luxurious mint-green hotel room in Oxnard. She stood a few feet inside the door and simply stared. There were two queen-size beds on a raised dais to her left. To her right was a bathroom and next to that a wet bar and a small refrigerator. Directly in front of her was a separate sitting area with a couch, coffee table and television set. Beyond that was a huge balcony and through the open curtains of the sliding-glass doors, she could see the twinkling lights on the boats in the marina three stories below.

"Wow!" she exclaimed. "How did you know about a place like this? Have you been here before?"

"Yes." Jeff dropped their overnight cases inside the closet and shrugged out of his jacket. "Like it?"

"It's absolutely beautiful."

"I came here once for a transportation seminar," he explained. "It's a resort, you know. The place has everything. Tennis courts, heated pools and a fabulous restaurant." He grinned and walked toward her. "But lolling in a hot tub with a bunch of beer-swilling truckers isn't my idea of romantic. So I swore I'd come back someday with someone special." He tugged her into his arms and dropped a gentle kiss on her forehead. "And you're very special."

Hannah smiled tremulously. His grip tightened and one of his hands moved to stroke slowly over her hip. She shivered. They were going to make love. "I need to change," she murmured, her voice sounding muffled against his shirt.

He lifted her chin and raised her lips to meet his. The kiss was gentle and sweet, just the bare brush of his tongue against hers before he pulled away leaving her gasping and hungry for more.

Confused, she looked at him but he only smiled and began edging both of them back toward the bed. He kept his hands firmly around her waist as he sank down onto the mattress. "No," he countered huskily, "you don't need to change."

Jeff trapped her between his spread legs. She glanced down and saw the taut fabric of his jeans molded against the fullness of his loins. His hands slid down her legs and closed around the hem of her dress.

"Jeff," she said breathlessly as a thrill of anticipation shot through her. "What are you doing?"

Instead of answering, he leaned forward and buried his face against her stomach. She could feel his warm breath tickling her skin. "I want to undress you." His voice was thick, guttural. Tilting his head, he looked up, his eyes gleaming with desire. "Let me."

Hannah couldn't speak. Dumbly she nodded, silently giving him permission to do with her as he pleased.

Slowly, agonizingly slowly, he shoved the material up her thighs. She heard the sharp intake of his breath as the tops of her ivory stockings and the lacy garter belt holding them up were revealed to his gaze.

She felt him go still. Then suddenly he stood and whipped the dress over her head. Her eyes opened. A blush crept up her cheeks and her heart skipped a beat when she saw the way he was staring at her.

Jeff stood frozen, his gaze locked on her scantily clad body. His mouth was open slightly, the pulse point in his temple throbbed visibly and his ragged breathing echoed the heavy drumbeats of her heart. She shifted nervously and tried to cross her arms over her breasts. But he grabbed her wrists and gently shoved her hands away.

"No," he ordered urgently. "It gives me pleasure to look at you. Let me." He gulped air. "My God, I thought you were beautiful before, but in that outfit . . . you're like a living fantasy."

The sight of her standing less than six inches from him wearing nothing more than those sexy little scraps of lace made him so hard he ached. "Dear God in heaven," he whispered reverently. "It's a good thing I've got a strong heart."

The brief demicups of her ivory lace bra barely covered her creamy breasts and did nothing to hide her rosy-pink nipples. He swallowed and slid his gaze down the silky curve of her stomach to the tiny matching lace panties and garter belt.

He'd planned on going slowly—undressing her and then teasing them both until they couldn't stand it anymore. Every night for the past three weeks he'd been haunted by long, erotic and painfully real dreams of making love to her. Now he didn't know if he could wait.

"Jeff," she pleaded. She wanted him to touch her, to hold and kiss her. Make love to her. "Please."

He grabbed the bedclothes and sent them flying to the foot of the bed. Bending slightly, he scooped her up in his arms and laid her gently on the snowy-white sheets.

Kneeling on the mattress, he bent his head to take her mouth. He kissed her passionately, moving his tongue deep inside her mouth as he learned the taste of her again.

He loomed over her, a hand on each side of her head. Hannah felt wonderfully, deliciously trapped. Hot, sweet ecstasy flooded her as their tongues touched and stroked and tangled in an erotic dance.

Her fingers moved to the buttons of his plaid shirt, but he shifted quickly and captured her hands against his chest. Lifting his head, he glanced at her flushed face and smiled with satisfaction. Her lips were softly parted and her eyes wide and glazed with passion. Still keeping her hands flat against his breastbone, he bent and kissed her hard and fast. Jeff moved her hands back to her sides. "Lie still," he commanded softly.

"Jeff," she said, sounding bewildered. "Don't you want me to touch you?"

"Oh, yes," he said fervently. "I want you to touch me. I want you to kiss me, seduce me and drive me out of my mind. But not yet. Not this time."

He stared directly into her eyes. He wanted her to know exactly what he was giving tonight and—even more—what he was taking. "I'm going to do everything I've dreamed of doing to you since the first time I saw you. I'm going to take and take and take until I drain you dry, and then I'm going to give and give and give until I fill you completely."

Jeff was almost as shocked by what he'd said as she was. But he meant every word. After tonight, neither of them would have any doubts.

His hands moved to the clasp on the front of her bra and with shaking fingers he released the catch and peeled the material back. Cupping a soft breast in each hand, he rubbed his thumbs across the rosy peaks. They hardened instantly at his touch.

Hannah was on fire, his strange words forgotten as his fingers sent a surge of pleasure singing along her nerve endings. She moaned in the back of her throat and it turned into a whimper of frustration as she felt his hot mouth close over her nipple and draw it inside his mouth. One of his hands slid down her stomach and stroked her gently through the thin fabric of her panties.

Lying there seminude, she felt suddenly very vulnerable, very much at his mercy. His aggression thrilled her, called to something deep within her as she gave herself completely into his keeping. Dimly she realized he was taking control deliberately.

"I can't stand this," she whispered, wanting to touch him in return. Her arms clutched him around the neck. She needed him so badly she ached with it. "Please, please..."

"Soon," he murmured, moving to suckle her other breast. "Soon, sweetheart." He released the clips of her garters. "Lift up." She arched up and he freed her from the garter belt. Raising her shoulders, he pulled the bra off and tossed it onto the floor. Then he eased his fingers into her panties and slowly slid them down her hips.

Rising slightly, she started to take off her stockings but he gently shoved her flat against the mattress. "My stockings," she protested.

"I'll take them off." He pulled them down her legs, his fingers trailing erotically on the sensitive flesh between her thighs. Instinctively her hips arched, seeking more of his touch. He smiled, dropped the hose on the floor and then kissed her ankles.

Another ragged cry escaped from her half-parted lips as he kissed his way back up her legs. He nibbled her knees and nipped gently on the insides of her thighs. He was relentless, and she was going to die if he didn't enter her soon.

Jeff shuddered. The feel of her flesh beneath his hands and mouth, the scent of her perfume, her soft cries and moans and her incredible responsiveness were driving him wild. He had to have her, had to be inside her. Now.

He stood and began tearing off his clothes. "I was going to take it slow," he told her. "I wanted to make it last all night. But I can't."

Freed of his shirt and shoes, he shoved down his jeans and briefs and stepped out of them. She stared at him in wonder. He was hard and ready—his need as great as her own.

Hannah held out her arms. The bed dipped as he lowered his weight to her. He took her mouth in a long, searing kiss as he gently nudged her thighs apart. She was warm and moist and welcoming.

He started to move on top of her, then paused and reached over the side of the bed. She could hear him scrambling inside the pocket of his jeans, and the crackle of a little foil packet told her he'd found what he was looking for.

Jeff rolled away from her for a moment. "Hannah," he whispered insistently. She gazed up at him through slitted eyes. He planted a hand on each side of her and watched her carefully. His eyes were deep pools of raw desire; his chest was rapidly rising and falling with each ragged breath. "Look at me."

Slowly, carefully, Jeff eased inside her. She whimpered softly and he froze. But the feel of her hot, velvet flesh enfolding him was too much. He started to move. He groaned, wanting to take it slowly, to make it last.

But Hannah had other plans.

Her excitement rose to fever pitch as she watched him struggle to hold back, felt his muscles bunching beneath her fingers. She lifted against him, sighing as the sudden movement pulled him deeper within her. His eyes grew wild, his expression fierce. Gasping, he looked into her eyes and saw his own savage desire mirrored in her gaze. His control snapped. He slipped his hands beneath her hips and lifted her tightly against him. "Wrap your legs around me," he commanded.

Too far gone to do anything but heed the driving urges racking her body, she willingly obeyed. Jeff was beyond thinking, beyond anything except feeling, being inside her, merging with her.

The connection grew tighter, the pressure unbearable as he drove steadily into her; mating, bonding, forging them into one entity. He thrust hard and fast, taking them higher and higher until he felt her shuddering beneath him and heard her soft cries of fulfillment. Her release drove him over the edge. For an infinite moment, white-hot pleasure gripped his entire body. He let go and rode the crest of release. Then he surrendered to the most blissful peace he'd know in three weeks.

In the aftermath of their lovemaking, they slept heavily. Jeff woke first but he kept his eyes closed, enjoying the feel of Hannah's warm silky body snuggled next to him. She was cuddled against his chest, sleeping on her side, with his arm draped loosely about her waist.

He opened his eyes and looked at her. She was deeply asleep, breathing slowly and evenly. Waking next to her seemed the most natural thing in the world.

He silently vowed that soon, he'd be doing it every morning of his life.

Hannah stirred with a languorous movement that caused her to brush her hip against his groin. Gently he shifted, and rolled her onto her back. In the shadowy morning sunlight filtering in through the closed drapes, he gazed at her for a long time. She was so beautiful—her face, her body, her spirit and her character. And she was his now.

Leaning on one elbow, he kissed her neck and tickled its pulse point with his tongue. She sighed. Sliding downward, he kissed his way over the soft mounds of her breast and took a nipple into his mouth. She moaned.

He made love to her gently, tenderly, easing them both into ecstasy before she was even properly awake—the perfect way to start the day.

Waking up in Jeff's arms eased the inevitable awkwardness of the "morning after" for Hannah. Too content to move, she pulled the covers around herself and buried her face in the pillow.

"Hey, sweetheart—" he shook her shoulder "—don't go back to sleep on me. There's something I have to ask you."

"If you're going to ask me if it was good for me—" she yawned "—don't bother. It was wonderful."

"I'm not deaf, dumb and blind." He chuckled, dropping a kiss on her shoulder. "If you'd moaned any louder the neighbors would have called the manager."

Hannah's eyes flew open. "Oh, my God," she said, mortified. "Was I that loud?"

"Not really," he soothed. "Just enough to inflate my ego bigger than a 747." He hugged her hard, laughing at the blush on her face. "But I was going to ask what you wanted for breakfast. They have terrific room service here."

"I'll have ham and eggs," she replied, tossing the covers off and climbing out of bed. At the bathroom door she turned and grinned saucily. "Why don't you order some humble pie?" He threw a pillow at her.

After feasting on ham, eggs and a pot of coffee, they spent the morning swimming and sunning. In the afternoon they went sight-seeing in nearby Solvang, California's little Denmark.

When they drove back to the coast, Jeff turned north and headed toward Ventura. "Let's find a nice beach and take a walk," he suggested. Hannah readily agreed.

The sun had disappeared behind the clouds and a misty afternoon fog rolled in off the Pacific as Jeff pulled into the parking lot of the state beach. The silence he'd maintained since leaving Solvang was beginning to wear on Hannah. She watched him out of the corner of her eye as they climbed a sand dune and headed for the hard-packed sand by the surf.

When they reached the water's edge, he took her by the shoulders and turned her to face him. "We need to talk."

She stiffened and her stomach twisted in dread. She'd known this was coming. They'd had a perfect day. For a few hours she'd pretended they were just ordinary lovers, two people enjoying a quiet weekend together. But that wasn't true. She and Jeff faced a host of problems, but she'd been hoping she wouldn't have to think about them quite yet. She should have known better. "What about?"

"The way you left."

Startled, she widened her eyes. "But I already explained."

He shook his head. "You explained what you were feeling, but that's only part of the story. I want to know why my being grateful scared you so much."

"I didn't say it scared me," she protested, not sure she liked being thought a coward.

He looked skeptical. "Okay, maybe it didn't scare you, but you've got to admit your reaction was hardly normal. I try to thank you for saving my sister's life, and you take off like a bat out of hell." He draped his arm over her shoulder and pulled her to his side as they started walking.

Hannah kept her gaze straight ahead. She didn't want to look at him—because she knew she'd have to tell him about Kevin; about why being with a grateful man frightened the devil out of her.

"Sweetheart," he continued carefully, "I know there's more to the story. I want to know what was going through your mind, why you felt so strongly about it that you left."

Hannah closed her eyes for a long moment and leaned her head against his shoulder. They stopped and she could feel him watching her. When she lifted her head and looked at him, his expression was determined.

"You're right," she said with a sigh. "There *is* more to it." She took a deep breath and told him about Kevin Webster.

Once she started, the words poured out. Hannah didn't even notice when they started walking again. By the time she'd finished her story, she was drained.

"That bastard."

"Kevin wasn't a bastard," Hannah explained hastily as she stopped and turned to Jeff. "He just didn't love me."

Jeff's jaw tightened. "Like hell," he snarled softly. "That little creep used you. He took advantage of your feelings for him and got six months of free nursing care for his mother."

"No," she argued, not sure if she was defending Kevin or herself. "You've got it wrong. Kevin wasn't deliberately taking advantage of me. It just happened that way. We started dating before his mother got sick."

"But I bet he didn't get serious until after he found out just how sick Mama was," Jeff shot back angrily. He wasn't mad at Hannah, but it was so clear to him exactly what that man had done to her. He was amazed she couldn't see it.

Hannah drew back. She looked confused for a moment and chewed on her lower lip. "You're right," she admitted, astonished. "He didn't get serious with me till after his mother was sick."

"Oh, baby." Jeff pulled her close and crushed her against his chest. He stared skyward and focused on a circling gull. "I'm not trying to dredge up painful memories. I'm trying to make you understand that a man doesn't make love to a woman the way I make love to you because he feels grateful." His grip tightened and Hannah squeaked. He eased his hold and stepped back, keeping her at arm's length. "Do you see what I'm saying?" he pleaded. "You're a loving, giving woman. He didn't even have to know you particularly well to figure that out. What really happened ten years ago is that you got taken advantage of. Look at the facts. One, he didn't get serious until after his mother was diagnosed. Two, Kevin didn't drop out of school to handle the nursing chores—he convinced you to cut *your* class load. And, three, when his mother died he started two-timing you."

Hannah stared at him thoughtfully. She wished she could believe him. But he was wrong. It hadn't been that way. Kevin was a kind and decent man who hadn't realized what he was feeling until it was too late. For part of their relationship, he'd genuinely thought he cared for her—it was only later that he understood he was just feeling grateful. But Jeff couldn't accept that. "Well, maybe..."

"No 'maybe' about it. The guy was just a user." His eyes narrowed somberly. "But I'm not a user, Hannah. This is for real."

"I hope so," she said with a sad smile.

"Come on," he urged, catching her hand and pulling her up the beach. "No more serious stuff—at least not for today. Let's walk off all those calories we ate."

The rest of the weekend was carefree and wonderful. They swam, talked, and made love repeatedly.

On Sunday, Jeff insisted on a late checkout so they could take one last dip in the pool.

Hannah was sitting with her eyes closed, her head lolling against the side of the hot therapy pool. Jeff sat across from her.

"What's the next step?" he asked suddenly.

Hannah lifted her head and stared at him. "What do you mean?"

He sighed. "I want more than just a weekend romance," he stated bluntly. He looked away from her. Through the steam rising from the water, she could see his expression was hard and unyielding.

Surprised, Hannah wasn't sure how she was supposed to answer. Did he want her to quit her job and move to San Francisco? "I want more than an occasional weekend, too," she agreed hesitantly. "You said you came down to San Diego a lot on business," she reminded him pointedly. "And I can easily fly up to see you. You're the one who claimed we could work things out."

"I suppose that'll have to do for right now," he muttered grudgingly. "Are you going to tell your mother about me?"

"Of course," she answered lightly. "You're too big to hide in my closet. I suppose I'll have to tell her sometime."

"When?"

"Do you want the exact date and time?"

"Yes."

"Jeff, why are you doing this? Why are you trying to ruin what's been the best weekend of my life?"

He moved abruptly and swung around, putting an arm along each side of her. "Because," he said in a low, gritty voice, "I want it all. I won't let you pretend we're nothing more than weekend lovers. Neither of us is footloose and fancy-free. We have a lot of other people in our lives, and the only way we can be together is openly and honestly. I won't have you pretending I don't exist for five days a week and then sneaking off to meet me when your mother's back is turned."

She stared at him coolly. "I gave up sneaking around when I was eighteen."

"I'm sorry, baby. That was unfair." He raked his hand through his damp hair. "But this is only going to work if we're both completely honest with our families."

"What are you saying?" she asked in a painful whisper.

"I want to meet Mary, and I want you to meet my family."

Chapter Twelve

"Don't look so worried, honey," he soothed, seeing her stricken expression. "I wasn't suggesting you do it right this second." He smiled tenderly and brushed a stray curl from her temple. "But I do want you to meet them soon. Both of us are too devoted to our families to have any kind of important relationship without including them."

Hannah slumped against the side of the pool. His words rang true, but that didn't make them any easier to accept. She closed her eyes, thinking of all the holidays and birthdays and family get-togethers that couples automatically shared.

"I suppose you're right," she whispered. There was a sinking feeling in the pit of her stomach. He sounded so sure, so confident, so absolutely certain of the future. But she was scared. And the horrible thing was, she didn't know why.

He stood to face her, pulling her up against him and brushing a kiss over her closed eyelids. "Don't fret, sweetheart," he assured her. "I'm not asking you to host a formal dinner party for your mother and my parents tomorrow night. I'll give you some time. I'll give us both some time. Working out a long-distance love affair won't be easy." Nor would it be practical in the long run, he thought quickly, but it would do for right now. "Still, we can handle it. Together, we can handle anything."

Hannah quivered, and Jeff's grip tightened around her arms.

"Look at me," he commanded softly. Her eyes fluttered open and she lifted her gaze to meet his. His expression was determined, as though he were willing her to believe him. "There's no need to panic. I said I'd give you time."

Jeff's last word finally registered in Hannah's brain.

"How much time?" she asked quickly, and then cursed herself for sounding so eager.

His eyes narrowed speculatively. "I said I wouldn't rush you," he replied bluntly. "But I'd rather not wait forever."

Wanting to placate him, she smiled and wrapped her arms around his waist. "You won't have to wait forever," she promised, leaning close and running her tongue across his nipple. She heard a low rumble deep in his chest as the small nub tightened, and she shivered in response, almost forgetting she was trying to distract him.

"Just give me a little space—I need to adjust to having a lover," she said softly as she stroked her hands up the taut muscles of his arms. "Then I'll tell my mother. I promise."

She moved fully against him, molding her femininity flush against his manhood and rhythmically thrusting against his flesh. Jeff shuddered violently.

"Ah, baby," he growled, "when you touch me like that I think I'd give you anything."

She gazed at him through half-closed eyes, her body suddenly on fire as he hardened instantly against her, fueling her excitement and making her forget they were in a public place. But Jeff hadn't forgotten.

She cried out in frustration as he stepped away, breaking the intimate contact. He reached for her and pulled them both out of the pool. "Come on," he said enthusiastically, grabbing a towel and tossing one to her. "Let's get back to the room. We've got at least an hour before we have to check out."

Hannah felt like a complete fraud. Three weeks had passed since she'd promised Jeff she'd tell her mother about their relationship, and she hadn't said one word.

He hadn't pushed her. For the past three weeks he'd been patient, gentle and very, very loving. When she'd flown to meet him in San Francisco, he hadn't insisted she meet the Kenyons. Last weekend, Jeff had been in Los Angeles on business and she'd met him there. Even then, he hadn't said a word. But this weekend was different. She had the feeling her time was running out.

Disgustedly Hannah shrugged and tossed aside the magazine she'd been trying to read. Jeff had out-and-out demanded she do as she'd promised. She threw a quick glare in the direction of the bathroom. He was still in the shower.

Since she'd picked him up at the airport on Friday night, he'd made it clear that not only did he expect her to tell Mary about him right away, but he expected her to meet his family soon.

Hannah wasn't scared anymore. She was angry, resentful and terrified. Jeff was trying to force their relationship to a different level. A deeper level, one that touched every aspect of her life. He was trying to bind her to him not just as a weekend lover, but through family ties that linked them together through their half sister and her birth mother. He was that kind of a man—the kind who wanted her to share his life in every possible way. But the risk to her was too high. One day, his gratitude would wear off and he'd casually expect her to be able to handle the fact that he didn't care anymore. Oh, he'd still like her as a person, probably even want to be friends. But he wouldn't really care. And then where would she be?

She'd be in a relationship with her birth relatives that would hurt her mother and, even worse, force her to be around him when it was all over between them. The thought of seeing Jeff when he no longer needed or wanted her was too painful to be borne.

"What time is it?" Jeff called from behind the closed door.

With a start she realized the water in the shower had stopped running. "Six," she shouted. "But don't worry, you've still got plenty of time to make your plane."

The phone rang. Hannah hurriedly snatched it up, hoping it wasn't her mother. "Hello."

"Well, hi, honey," Mary said with a laugh. "I didn't expect to find you home—you've been gone so much these past few weekends. But I thought I'd try anyway."

"Hi, Mom." She glanced at the bathroom door. "I thought you were going to the Mission Rally with John at Newport Beach this weekend."

"We did go," Mary exclaimed. "We got back about four this afternoon. You know those things always end directly after worship service. My goodness, you do have your head in the clouds these days."

Hannah forced a laugh. "You're right, I forgot."

"That's okay, dear. I've had my head in the clouds a lot, too, lately," Mary said cheerfully. "I'm calling to remind you about the engagement party next Saturday. I need to borrow those lace tablecloths your great-aunt Hilda gave you. Is that all right?"

"That'll be fine," Hannah answered quickly, wanting to get off the line before Jeff came out.

"Good. I'll pick them up tomorrow evening."

Hannah frowned. "I may not be here, so just use your key and come on in."

"You're not going to be working late again, are you?" her mother chided. "That's not good for you. Goodness gracious, I know you're devoted to your job, but—"

"Mom," Hannah interrupted, wanting to nip Mary's lecture in the bud, "I'm not working. I'm going shopping with Kim."

"I'm sorry," Mary said ruefully. "I didn't mean to nag."

"It's okay. Anyway, the tablecloths are on the top shelf in the linen closet. Help yourself."

"I'll do that." Mary hesitated. "Are you going to be bringing someone special to the party?"

The party. Hannah cringed as it hit her that her mother's engagement party was next Saturday night. What was she going to do? What could she tell Jeff when he started making plans for next weekend? Oh, hell! Why was life so complicated?

"Hannah?"

"What...oh sorry, Mom." She took a deep breath. The urge to say yes was overwhelming. But she firmly clamped down on the word as it hovered on the tip of her tongue. She wasn't going to say one word about Jeff until after her mother's wedding. Nothing was going to spoil Mary's happiness. "No," she said quietly. "I won't be bringing anyone."

Mary sighed and then laughed. "I suppose you'll tell me what you're up to in your own good time. I've got to run now. Take care, and I'll see you Saturday night."

Hannah stared at the receiver for a few seconds, wondering if she was doing the right thing. She wasn't cut out to live a lie, and her mother obviously knew something important was happening in her life.

"Who was that on the phone?"

Hannah jumped and whirled around. Jeff stood in the doorway. A towel wrapped around his waist, his hair wet, he was staring at her with an assessing gaze that made her flush guiltily.

"A friend," Hannah lied. She smiled brilliantly and asked, "Do you want to pack now or do you want to have a bite to eat first?"

His mouth flattened to a thin line. "What friend?"

Guilt mushroomed inside her, then expanded into self righteous anger. "Jeff," she said, trying hard to make her tone flippant, "what is this? The third degree? What's gotten into you?"

He shrugged. "Sorry," he muttered, not sounding in the least sorry. "I suppose I'm feeling a little insecure these days. I've had the feeling lately that you're not taking this relationship seriously."

"That's not true," she protested. Hannah couldn't meet his eyes anymore. She bent over and began picking up the newspapers strewn over the coffee table. "Of course, I take us seriously. What's wrong with you?"

He crossed his arms over his chest. "Nothing's wrong with me. But your reluctance to mention me to the person most important to you leads me to believe you don't care about how I feel."

Still not meeting his eyes, she said, "Of course, I care about how you feel. Just because I haven't found the right moment to mention you to my mother doesn't mean I don't value our relationship."

"Hannah," he said softly, his tone serious, "I'm not accusing you of anything. I'm just asking a question."

"I don't understand what you're getting at."

"What I'm getting at?" Jeff sighed. "I guess I'm asking you just how important I really am to you."

She looked up and saw the uncertainty and the worry in his face and she couldn't stand it. Flying across the room, Hannah hurled herself into his arms. "Forgive me," she pleaded. "Of course, you're important to me. If it means that much to you, I'll tell her this week. I promise."

She looked up and he gave her a strained smile. "I don't want to push you," he murmured. "But we can't go on this way." Jeff took a deep breath. "I know that was your mother on the phone—wasn't it?"

Hannah couldn't lie again. She nodded.

He sighed against the top of her head. "I wasn't eavesdropping, but I heard you when I came out to get my shaving kit from the bedroom."

She winced and buried her face against his chest.

"I want you in my life completely," he continued. "And I want to be completely in yours. But the only way we can do that is by being open and honest with each other." His voice dropped to a harsh whisper. "I want to tell my parents and Kirsten about our being together. I want to share the birthdays and the holidays and the problems and the pain, and take you for long weekends at my folks' beach house. I want to do everything with you. But you're making that impossible and I don't know how much longer I can keep this up." He gave her a small shake. "The company's having their annual dinner dance in two weeks. Irene and Reece will be there. I'll have to be there, and damn it, I want you with me."

She smiled sadly. He wanted her with him now; but that wasn't the point. "Now" wouldn't last forever; and one day, he wouldn't need her at all. Hannah tightened her arms around his waist and pressed against him. She'd give him the words he wanted to hear because she couldn't stand the pain in his voice. "I'll tell Mom this week," she said quietly. "I promise."

Jeff didn't reply for a long moment; he just held her tightly and rested his chin on the top of her head.

"I believe you," he finally responded. Loosening from her grip, he stepped away, hitching up his towel as he walked to the bedroom. "I'm sorry, honey. I didn't mean to end our weekend with an argument. I suppose I'm a little jumpy because I'm worried about Kirsten."

"Kirsten." Hannah's heart leaped into her throat. "Wait a minute!" she yelped, following him into the bedroom. "Why didn't you tell me there was something wrong?"

"There's nothing really wrong," he said, reaching for his pants. "She's picked up a mild infection. But don't worry. She's responding to the antibiotics, and the doctor doesn't think there's any need for alarm." He pulled up his zipper and turned to face her. She'd paled and her eyes were wide with alarm.

"Hey," he said gently, crossing the room and pulling Hannah into his arms. "Take it easy. Kirsten's going to make it. I was just uptight because we've had such smooth sailing since the transplant. It's only a little setback, not a full-scale catastrophe."

"You're sure?" She swallowed painfully against the fear.

"I'm sure." He hugged her close and brushed a kiss on the top of her head. "Don't you remember? You're the one who convinced me she's going to make it. I believe that now, and I want you to believe it, too."

Hannah did believe Kirsten would be fine. But she was beginning to have serious doubts about herself.

Neither of them referred to their argument on the way to the airport. Jeff steered Hannah's compact through the heavy freeway traffic, good-naturedly complaining that it drove worse than some of the company's old trucks.

Hannah was distracted, but she managed to respond to him enough to keep the conversation flowing.

He pulled up in front of the terminal and drew her close for long, lingering kiss. "I'll call you tomorrow

and we'll make plans for next weekend.'' Not waiting
for her to reply, he leaped out of the car, grabbed his
overnight bag from the back seat, and hurried off to
catch his plane.

Hannah cowardly put off calling Jeff and letting
him know she wasn't coming to San Francisco until
after she got home from work Tuesday night. He
hadn't called her on Monday as he'd promised and she
was a little relieved. She hated lying to him. But if she
mentioned Mary's engagement party, he'd want to
come; and she couldn't risk that. Not yet. Her mother
wasn't ready.

But she needn't have worried about telling Jeff
anything. When she dialed his number she got his answering machine. She left a brief message, telling him
she had to work over the weekend and then quickly
hung up.

For the rest of the week, they kept missing each
other. The only time she heard Jeff's voice was on her
answering machine. He told her he'd gotten her message and he'd call later in the week, but he never did.
Nor did he answer his phone.

By the time Saturday rolled around and Hannah
was getting ready for the party, she wished she'd called
him at work.

Hannah pulled her brand-new dress out of its protective plastic wrap and laid it on the bed. She bit her
lip, wondering if the dress was a bit too much for a
minister's engagement party, then shrugged her
shoulders and slipped it on anyway.

Stepping back, she examined herself critically in the
full-length mirror and sighed, wishing Jeff could see
her. The black velvet dress was spectacular. The

dropped neckline with its scalloped edge, the tucked waist and bell-shaped skirt all looked perfect.

But Jeff wouldn't see it. For a moment, she panicked, worried because she hadn't heard from him all week. But then she realized she was being silly. She wasn't the only one with a heavy workload. Jeff had already told her Kirsten's illness had put him way behind on the company's annual reports. Feeling more reassured, she finished getting ready for the party.

The festivities were in full swing when Hannah pulled up in front of John McMahon's hillside home. She'd never been there before, so she got out of the car and gazed curiously at the large two-story stucco house her mother would soon be moving into.

Lights blazing from the front of the house revealed a brick walkway leading across a lush green lawn and ending at a set of double doors with a huge brass knocker. Hannah smiled, feeling relieved. Her footsteps tapped merrily against the walk as she realized her mother was marrying a man who could take care of her.

John met her at the door and pulled her inside. "Come in. Come in, my dear," he said, dropping a kiss on her cheek. "We were wondering what was keeping you."

"I'm sorry I'm late," she replied, letting him lead her across a wine-colored carpet into a beautifully decorated English country-style living room. There were people scattered everywhere. Trying to find her mother, Hannah gazed around the room until she spotted Mary next to a baby-grand piano in the far corner. She was talking with a tall, dark-haired man whose back was turned toward Hannah.

"What would you like to drink?" John asked.

"White wine," she murmured with a smile. "I'll just go say hello to Mom," she called as the pastor left her to get the drink.

Smiling, Hannah started across the room, then stopped dead.

Jeff. Her mother was laughing and chatting with Jeff Kenyon as though they were old friends.

Stunned, Hannah stared at him as if he were Lazarus risen from the grave. At that moment, her mother glanced over and saw her.

"Hannah! There you are. We were wondering why you were so late."

Jeff turned and watched as she slowly crossed the room. Their eyes met and a blush of shame crept up her cheeks. He was smiling at her, but it didn't touch his eyes.

"Hello, Mother," Hannah said, kissing her mother's cheek. She added softly, "Hello, Jeff."

"Hannah—" his voice was clipped "—you're late. The party started an hour ago."

"I got held up," she explained hastily. My God, what on earth was happening? "What are you doing here?" she asked breathlessly. "I mean—" She broke off as he gave her another mirthless smile.

"Your mother invited me." His voice was soft and loaded with meaning.

Hannah winced and quickly looked away. It didn't take a genius to figure out what he was thinking. He was wondering why she hadn't invited him, and even worse, he probably realized that not only had she not told Mary about him, but she'd lied about being busy this weekend.

Mary glanced curiously from Jeff to Hannah. She cleared her throat, plastered a brilliant smile on her face and turned to her daughter. "Wasn't it lucky that Jeff called while I was getting those tablecloths at your place?" she chirped gaily, ignoring the thick tension that had suddenly engulfed them. "As soon as he introduced himself, why, I naturally invited him tonight. Hannah, shame on you! Keeping this nice young man a secret is a terrible thing to do to your poor mother. You know I've been dying for you to meet someone special."

Hannah groaned silently, thinking that after tonight, Jeff probably wouldn't be special to her much longer. She risked a glance at his face. He was smiling faintly at Mary.

Then it hit her. Her mother was treating Jeff as though he were the Prodigal Son. Maybe she didn't realize exactly who he was. Maybe she didn't understand that he was Kirsten's brother. But that notion was quickly dispelled when Mary reached across and touched Jeff's arm.

"How is your sister?" Mary asked, her eyes clouding in concern.

A real smile came into Jeff's eyes. "She's doing well. She had a bit of a setback last week, but that's over now. It looks like Hannah's bone marrow took, and every day Kirsten's white blood-cell count goes up. The doctor says if she keeps improving like this, she can go home in a few weeks."

Mary clasped her hands in front of her and grinned from ear to ear. "That's wonderful. I'm glad to hear it. Hannah's been so worried." She shook her head. "It must be miserable for a teenager to be cooped up in an isolation ward. I bet she's looking forward to going home."

"Kirsten will still be a little isolated," Jeff explained. "For the next few months she'll have to stick pretty close to home—we can't take the risk of her being exposed to crowds with her immunity levels so low. But it looks like she's got a real chance at beating this thing. Thanks for asking. I appreciate your concern."

"Of course, I was concerned," Mary said briskly. "Kirsten is, after all, Hannah's sister. I hope you won't be offended . . ." She hesitated and bit her lip.

The gesture was so much like Hannah that Jeff smiled. "What?"

"I don't know what your religion is," Mary continued with an apologetic shrug, "but as soon as I heard about Kirsten's leukemia, I put her on the prayer chain at my women's circle." She watched Jeff anxiously. "I hope you don't mind. John's always telling me that not everyone appreciates being prayed for. As a matter of fact, I prayed for an atheist once, and he got really annoyed. But I figured it wouldn't hurt, and I like to believe that maybe it helped."

Jeff gazed at Mary for what seemed an eternity, then he leaned down and kissed her on the cheek. "You can pray for Kirsten any time you want," he said softly. "That's the nicest thing I've ever heard. And having you for a mother, it's no wonder Hannah is such a giving person. She obviously got it from you."

Mary turned a bright pink and Hannah would have fallen over if she hadn't grabbed the top of the piano.

"Thank you," Mary replied. She smiled at Hannah. "I did do a pretty good job with her, didn't I?" Patting Jeff's arm lightly, she said, "Oh dear, Pastor Rheinhold's calling me. You two enjoy yourselves, now."

Mary hurried off and Hannah was left alone with Jeff. She took a deep breath and turned to face him. "I know you're upset—"

"*Upset* is too mild a word for what I'm feeling right now," he interrupted in a flat voice. "But we're here as your mother's guests. Whatever I have to say to you can wait until we get to your place."

The evening seemed to last forever. Jeff stayed close to her side, almost as though he were afraid that if he turned his back, she'd disappear.

Hannah smiled dutifully and introduced Jeff to the other guests, most of whom were members of her father's old congregation. She felt absolutely wretched inside, desperately wanting to be alone with Jeff so she could explain things, but simultaneously dreading it. What on earth could she say? She'd lied. Deceived him. And her reasons for doing so were evaporating as quickly as the ice in John's fruit punch. Sipping her wine, she turned and gazed across the room at her mother.

Smiling and chatting, Mary was obviously having the time of her life. Meeting Jeff hadn't upset her in the least.

Hannah couldn't believe she'd been so wrong. She risked a quick glance at Jeff. He was sipping a Scotch and listening politely to something John was saying.

He glanced up and their gazes collided. For a split second, his eyes blazed fiercely with an emotion she couldn't read, then he turned away.

Oh, God! she thought morosely, her heart sinking to her toes. He probably thinks I've been lying to him all along. Tears clogged her throat but she ruthlessly clamped her mouth shut, knowing she had to maintain control. Her mother's reaction to meeting Jeff had no doubt convinced him she'd been lying through her teeth. And she hadn't. But she had an awful feeling he'd never believe her now.

Jeff's hand tightened around her elbow as an elderly gentleman peered over her shoulder. Hannah had never been so glad to see anyone in her life. The instant Charles Blaine realized Jeff was in the transportation industry, he latched on to him like a limpet. Blaine Industries was always looking for a cheaper way to get their goods to market.

Breathing a sigh of relief, Hannah escaped and slipped out to the terrace. The February night was cold and cloudless but she didn't even feel the chill. She was too numb. She walked to the edge of the terrace and stared into the darkness.

How could she have been so wrong? Why was her mother reacting like this? What was Jeff thinking? Dear God, how on earth would she ever explain it? Her fingertips rubbed her temples while she tried to still the whirling, frightening questions.

Behind her the door opened, and without even turning she knew who it was.

"Hannah—" his voice was cold enough to frost the dew on the grass "—it's time to go."

He walked up behind her and then a moment later, his coat was draped over her shoulders. She hadn't brought a wrap of her own and she was grateful for its warmth. "Thank you," she murmured quietly.

"I've said your goodbyes," he continued. "I'll follow you home and then we can talk."

"Talk. You're willing to listen to me?" She turned to look at him and then wished she hadn't. His eyes were the color of blue frost.

"Of course, I'm willing to listen. You're important to me. The question is, how important am I to you?"

"Jeff," she began earnestly. He reached up and placed a finger on her lips.

"Not here," he growled. He handed her her purse, took her arm and led her around to the front of the house toward her car. They stopped by his rental car. "I'll follow you to your place. We're going to need privacy for this discussion."

She walked to her car, climbed in and started the engine. Jeff signaled for her to pull in front of him.

She lived less than five miles away, but for Hannah it was the longest drive of her life.

Chapter Thirteen

"Would you like some coffee?" Hannah called over her shoulder, her voice thick with tension. She heard the door shut with a soft click but she couldn't bring herself to turn around and face him.

"No," he replied flatly. "I don't want any coffee. I want to talk."

Hannah's stomach contracted painfully. Jeff didn't sound in any mood to be reasonable, but then she couldn't blame him. After all, she'd not only broken her promise, she'd lied, as well. Tossing her purse on the sofa, she took a deep breath and steeled herself for his wrath. "I know you're angry."

He snorted in disgust. "Angry?" he repeated mockingly. "I've got news for you, lady. That doesn't even come close to describing how I feel right now."

Gathering her courage, she turned and looked at him. "I wasn't lying.... I mean, I did work today and

I really did plan to tell her this week—'' She broke off and clasped her shaking hands together. ''But the timing wasn't right.''

Jeff stared at her stonily. He pushed away from the door and stalked toward her. ''You promised you'd tell Mary about us this week. You gave me your word. Do you have any idea how idiotic I felt when I called here the other night and she answered the phone? It was damned obvious she didn't know a thing about us.''

''But she invited you—''

''Yeah, *she* invited me.'' He stopped in front of her and she flinched at the hard, unyielding expression on his face. Jeff saw her reaction and knew he was hurting her. But he was in too much pain himself to care. ''Something *you* should have done. Why didn't you?''

''I was going to,'' she insisted, her eyes pleading with him to understand. ''But she's been so happy, and I was afraid that knowing about you would upset her.''

Hannah watched him carefully, praying she'd see a glimmer of understanding and compassion cross his face. He stared back at her silently, his jaw rigid and his eyes glittering like chips of blue ice. ''I decided it would be better to wait until after the wedding,'' she finished lamely.

He laughed harshly. ''Sure. And then you'd have decided to wait until after the honeymoon and then until after she was all settled in.... When were you *really* planning on telling her? When she collected her first social-security check?'' He broke off and clenched his hands into fists.

''I'm sorry.''

Exhaling a long breath, he raked a hand through his hair and brought himself under control. "Believe it or not," he said in a chillingly calm voice, "so am I."

The utter finality of his tone sent her heart pounding in panic. Oh, God! she thought frantically. He doesn't care anymore. "Jeff," she pleaded, "let me explain."

He didn't reply. He merely turned his back on her and walked over to stare out the window into the dark night.

Hannah was so shaken she couldn't speak for a second. Didn't he even want to listen to her? Didn't he care enough to give her a chance?

"All right," he said gravely, not looking at her. "Why don't you explain it to me. Help me understand."

She took a step toward him but then stopped when she saw him stiffen. "I only wanted to give my mother some time. I swear it."

"Your mother... or you?" he asked skeptically.

"What do you mean by that?" She hated talking to his back, but she didn't have the nerve to ask him to turn around.

"You've had weeks, but you haven't done it. What were you waiting for? Were you hoping you could convince me to drift along as we were? Seeing each other on weekends and pretending for the rest of the time that we didn't exist?"

"No!"

"Yes!" he insisted. He started pacing back and forth in front of the window, but he still didn't look at her. "The problem isn't Mary," he muttered thoughtfully, almost as though he were talking to himself. "The problem is you. You've been looking for an excuse to avoid making a real emotional commitment to our relationship." He stopped and swiveled his head to stare at her.

"That's not true!" she protested. "Besides, what does that have to do with my not telling my mother about you? Our relationship has nothing to do with that."

"Doesn't it?" Jeff asked. Moving swiftly, he came over to stand in front of her. Unable to endure the accusation in his eyes, Hannah dropped her gaze to the floor. "Tell me the truth, Hannah," he continued, his voice a quiet, compelling whisper. "Weren't you planning on being busy for the next few weekends? Your mother's wedding is a great excuse. Even I couldn't complain if you had to stay here and help her get ready for it. Weren't you hoping that by the time we were together again, I'd be so damned glad to have you back in my arms, I'd stop pressuring you?" His hands came up and clasped her shoulder. "You're a bright lady. You know how crazy I am about you. Admit it. If you stalled off long enough, you knew I'd be so happy to see you I wouldn't want to do anything to upset you. And I sure as hell wouldn't insist on dragging you off for a weekend with the Kenyon clan."

Hannah opened her mouth to tell him he was wrong, but the words died on her lips. Her head spun dizzily and her heart pounded frantically as the truth of what he'd said slammed into her with the force of a tornado.

She gulped air into her lungs, trying to calm herself. In the back of her mind, she'd been hoping for exactly the kind of scenario he'd described. But she hadn't realized it till now.

Shocked to her core, she stared blindly at her feet as a wave of self-disgust welled up in her throat and threatened to choke her. She could see the meaning behind her evasions and subterfuges with crystal clarity; and her self-deception made her sick.

"And then you'd have found another excuse, and then another until finally, I just gave up." He shook her gently. "That's it, isn't it! That eventually I'd just get tired of banging my head against a brick wall and accept what little of yourself you were prepared to give me."

She tried to speak—to deny his accusations—but she couldn't. She couldn't lie anymore. Not to herself and not to him.

"Hannah—" he cupped his hand under her chin and forced her to meet his gaze "—look at me."

She swallowed hard, knowing that in his eyes she was already condemned. But when their gazes met, instead of contempt and disgust, his eyes shone with compassion and...something else. Something she couldn't identify.

For a long moment, she simply stared at him. "I don't understand," she moaned in confusion. "Aren't you angry with me anymore?"

"No," he said gently. "I'm not mad. Not now. I'll admit when I saw you come waltzing into the party, I felt like turning you over my knee. But that was just a gut reaction. Once I calmed down, I realized that yelling at you wouldn't get us anywhere. I want to understand, Hannah. I want to know why you're so afraid of letting me completely into your life."

"But you are in my life," she insisted. "You're very important to me. I want to be with you."

"But not enough to invite me to your mother's engagement party." He shook his head. "That's a major event in a person's life. Yet you deliberately avoided mentioning it. Why?"

"But I've explained why I didn't say anything—"

"Yes," he interrupted. "You've explained and I think you've actually managed to convince yourself your reasons were valid. But that doesn't explain why you're withholding yourself from me."

There was a quality in his voice that sent a trickle of unease down her spine. She stiffened but didn't pull away. "What do you mean by that?"

Jeff closed his eyes for a moment and took a deep breath, steeling himself to take the biggest risk of his life. If he was wrong, he might lose her forever.

"Tonight's hassle isn't about meeting families," he said. "It's about you. About how you feel inside." He shook his head. "The problem isn't your mother's hang-up about birth families, and I think you know it."

She did pull away then. "I really thought her knowing about you would upset her."

"I'm sure that's what you told yourself. But be honest. Once the initial shock had worn off, your mother handled things fine. After learning about Kirsten, look what she did. She took off for Mexico and then got engaged to be married. That's not the behavior of a woman on the edge of a nervous breakdown... and if you'd stopped and thought about it, you'd have realized that." He cocked his head and studied her face. "You're deliberately not letting me get close. You're holding back emotionally, relegating our relationship to nothing more than weekend fun and games."

"That's not true." A cold, clammy fear took root in the pit of Hannah's stomach. "You don't know what you're talking about," she said hoarsely. "Having a bachelor's degree in psychology doesn't make you an expert on me." Jerking away, she turned and headed for her room. But before she's taken a step, he pulled her against him, slipped his arms around her waist and locked her tightly against his chest. "Let me go!" she commanded.

But Jeff ignored her and continued speaking.

"I didn't say I was an expert on you," he persisted. "But for God's sake, I don't have to be hit on the head with a two-by-four to understand. You've evaded taking any steps toward letting either of us really share each other's lives. And there's got to be a reason for that."

Something snapped inside Hannah. All the pain and the worry and the fear suddenly boiled over until she couldn't keep it inside anymore. She pulled away and whirled around to face him, her eyes blazing. "Okay I'll tell you the truth if that's what you want to hear."

He went still. "I do."

"You want a reason?" She smiled bitterly. "You don't want me to share your life. You want a lifeline—an anchor, a warm body who understands what you've been going through and is willing to help you cope with the pain. Remember me, Jeff? I'm the one who gave your sister a second chance. I'm the one who held you in my arms when the going got too much for you to stand and you couldn't hide your agony a minute longer. And you're grateful for that. You're grateful I gave Kirsten a few millimeters of bone marrow and you're grateful I was there when you needed me. But let's not kid ourselves anymore. Once you stop being grateful, you won't need me for a damn thing!''

"How can you think that?" He took a step toward her but she held up her hand.

"I don't think it. I *know* it." She gave a high-pitched laugh. "Right now, you've convinced yourself I'm important to you, and I am. But not as a woman you care about, not as a woman you could ever want for the long haul."

His eyes blazed with fury. "So we're back to that, are we? I thought we'd already solved that particular problem."

Overcome with anguish, she closed her eyes for a moment. "I wish to God we had," she whispered. "But all the talking in the world won't change the facts."

"So what you're saying is that you don't trust me to know my own feelings." He clenched his hands into fists.

"You won't mean to hurt me," she said stonily, refusing to look at him. "*Kevin* didn't mean to hurt me. But one day you'll wake up and you'll realize that you don't care about me. And if I do what you ask—if I get involved with Kirsten and Irene—I'll have to face you again and again." Her eyes filled with tears. "And I can't bear that."

She heard him draw a long, deep breath.

"Hannah," he said, his voice low and earnest, "I don't know what I can say to convince you. Maybe there aren't enough words in the English language for me to get through to you. But you're absolutely wrong. If I didn't know how much pain you were in, I'd be really angry that you have such a low opinion of me."

She shook her head furiously. "You don't get it, do you? I *don't* have a low opinion of you. You're a kind, decent, wonderful man. It would be so easy for you to pretend you know what you're doing, that everything would work out fine, because at the moment, you really believe you care for me. But don't you see? So did Kevin. It was only later, once the crisis was past, that he understood he didn't."

"Don't compare me to that user," Jeff snapped. "I *do* care about you."

"That's what Kevin thought, too!" she yelled. She broke off, appalled at herself for losing control. She closed her eyes and rubbed her forehead. "I think you'd better go."

"No." Jeff walked over and stood in front of her. "I've got something left to say, and I'm not leaving until you hear it."

"What is it?" she asked wearily, fighting the urge to dissolve in tears."

"I love you and I want to marry you." He looked at her. His face was open and vulnerable, his eyes pleading for her trust.

Hannah stared at him, wishing with all her might that she could believe him. A bittersweet, painful ache spread from her heart through her whole body. At this moment, he probably meant what he was saying. But this moment wouldn't last. One day, she'd have to watch him squirm uncomfortably every time she came into the same room; have to watch him avoid her eyes when she tried to talk to him, and have to hear him make excuses as to why he didn't want to make love to her. That's how it had been with Kevin at the end. She knew she couldn't stand to watch it end that way with Jeff. She wasn't that strong.

When she made no response to his declaration Jeff slumped against the wall. Neither of them spoke for a moment. Finally he straightened and put his hands on her shoulders. She stepped back and his hands fell limply to his sides. "Say something, damn it."

"There's nothing to say," she answered, her voice devoid of emotion.

"You're not willing to believe me, are you? Why? Why, Hannah?"

"I've told you why."

He stiffened against the surge of panic mushrooming in his stomach. After tonight, she wouldn't even be willing to see him on weekends. If he didn't get through to her, he'd lose her forever. Taking a deep breath, he brought himself under control, hoping against hope that he could find the right words to convince her to trust him.

"I love you Hannah, but I'm leaving now," he told her. "I'm walking out that door and going home. But I'll be waiting for you. For as long as it takes, I'll wait. When you think you can learn to believe me, to trust me, then give me a call and I'll come running." He swallowed hard. "But I'm not willing to have a weekend love affair with you. And the way things stand now, that's all we'll ever have."

Jeff slowly walked toward the front door, hoping with every step she'd say something. His hand closed over the knob and he paused for a second. He heard nothing but a painful silence. He ignored the fear clawing at his gut and turned to look at her one last time.

She stood frozen next to the sofa, her face ravaged and her eyes glazed and dull. For a moment, he considered going to her, but he knew if he did, they were doomed. Love without trust was worthless. And she had to learn to trust him on her own.

"Hannah," he said, his voice tender and soft, "I love you. But until you can really believe that, we've got nothing."

She looked away. A moment later she heard the door shut and knew he was gone.

She refused to believe him, to feel, to think. Despair, rage and agony flowed through her, twisting her into a tangled knot of painful threads. And each one pulled her in a different direction. Silent tears rolled down her cheeks and splashed onto the bare skin of her arm. She looked at them dismally.

The sight of her tears pooling against her skin caused the dam to finally break. With a low, keening moan of anguish, she fell to her knees and sobbed.

Hannah cried for hours—harder than she'd ever wept in her life. Eventually she didn't have any tears left. She went wearily to bed. But, exhausted as she was, she couldn't sleep.

All night his words haunted her, whispered to her from the darkened shadows of her room. Dawn had broken when she drifted into troubled sleep. But even that short respite was soon broken.

She was awakened by her mother shaking her shoulder. "Hannah, Hannah wake up. It's after one."

Opening her eyes, she saw Mary peering at her anxiously.

"Mom, what are you doing here?" She bolted up. "Is something wrong?"

"Everything's fine with me. But I was worried about you. You were supposed to meet me three hours ago. We were going to go over the wedding plans."

"Oh, yes. I forgot." Hannah brushed a lock of hair out of her eyes and stared down at the sheets. She knew her face was puffy and her eyes were swollen from crying.

"Jeff called me this morning. He's concerned. He told me the two of you had a rather... upsetting confrontation last night."

"Upsetting!" Hannah scoffed. "Is that how he described it?" She threw back the covers and swung her legs off the bed.

"I'll put a pot of coffee on," Mary said briskly. "You'll feel better when you've got something warm inside you."

Hannah dragged herself to the bathroom and got into the shower. But even the hot spray of the water beating against her skin wasn't enough to drive away the cold she felt within.

When she entered the kitchen, Mary was pouring coffee into mugs. "Hannah, I want to talk to you," she said handing her daughter her coffee. "There's something I've got to get off my chest, something that's been bothering me for months."

Hannah stared at her mother. "What?"

Mary wrapped her hands around her mug and sighed. "For years you believed I couldn't stand the idea of you even asking questions about your natural mother."

"Well, you did have a problem with that," Hannah muttered.

"Yes, when Hope was taken away, I'll admit I was crushed and I overreacted. But I could have gotten over it."

Hannah's head snapped up in amazement. "Then why didn't you?"

Mary pursed her lips. "I didn't have to."

"Mom, what are you saying?"

"I'm saying," Mary told her bluntly, "that I acted like a neurotic little fool and your father let me get away with it. Don't you think I know that you and your daddy used to hide newspapers and magazines from me if there was even one word about adoption in them? Don't you remember that one time you tried to ask me about your birth and I started carrying on and crying." She made a face of self-disgust. "I can't believe I was that selfish. And you and your daddy loved me enough to go along with it. But I've learned something lately. I've come to realize something very, very important. Something I paid lip service to for years."

"What?" Curious, Hannah stared at her mother.

Mary smiled. "Love isn't contingent on a tie of blood."

Hannah didn't know what to say, so she said nothing.

"I don't know what happened between you and Jeff," her mother continued softly, "but I do know that if you care about someone, you've got to take a few risks."

Take a few risks? No, she couldn't do that again. "I can't," she whispered raggedly. "I just can't."

The next few days passed in a mindless haze for Hannah and she threw herself into helping Mary plan her wedding. Neither woman referred to that fateful afternoon again, but Hannah was conscious of her mother watching her anxiously.

Jeff didn't call, and she couldn't bring herself to call him. She was too afraid—gripped by a mindless panic that was rooted deep inside her soul.

She was tormented constantly by images of Jeff and the things he'd said to her that night; and her mother's revelations had only added fuel to the inferno raging inside her. Mary had subtly told her that she could handle Hannah's meeting her birth family.

As she drove to work on Wednesday morning, she found herself thinking again and again of what her mother had said. Love did mean taking risks. But at what price? Her soul? Her sanity?

As she got out of her car, she spotted Leah Hofstadter sitting on the stairs by the front door.

"Hello, Leah," Hannah said warmly. "How are you feeling?"

"I'm fine." Leah nervously plucked at the material of her maternity top. She smiled shyly. "If you have a minute, I'd like to talk to you."

"Sure." Hannah paused on the steps while Leah pulled herself to her feet. "Would you like to go somewhere and sit down? We could go into my office."

"No, this won't take long." Leah brushed a lock of frizzy blond hair out of her eyes and took a deep breath. "I wanted to let you know I've decided to give the baby up."

Hannah was careful to hide her surprise.

"You've been so nice to me. You and Miss Weiner both," the teenager continued breathlessly. "I thought you'd want to know I've finally made up my mind."

"Are you comfortable with your decision?"

"Yes. I finally got it through my thick head that no one but me could make this decision." Leah's voice caught and her hazel eyes filled with tears. But she stood proudly, her chin lifted. "I love my baby. That's why I'm giving it up for adoption."

"I know this has been hard for you." Hannah smiled sympathetically.

Leah swiped at a tear and nodded. "Yes. But I can't give my baby a home. Look at me, Miss Breckenridge. I'm seventeen years old and I don't even have my high-school diploma yet. I can't give my baby what it deserves—a decent home and two parents who will love it." She stopped and drew in a shaky breath.

Hannah wanted to comfort Leah but she didn't have any magic words that would take the girl's pain away. "You sound like you've given this a lot of thought," she said softly. She didn't doubt that Leah loved her unborn child; the agony of her decision was reflected in her face. She looked ravaged but determined to do the right thing, no matter what the cost.

For the rest of the day, Hannah couldn't get Leah out of her mind. As she drove home that night, the girl's face haunted her all the way up the freeway. One part of her didn't want to acknowledge that Leah's giving up her child was the right course of action. But that was impossible. Leah genuinely loved her baby. She was only giving it away because she couldn't take care of it.

Without realizing it, Hannah began to wonder about why Irene had given her up. By the time she pulled into her parking space, she was thinking about the question as if it were the most natural thing in the world.

When she entered her apartment, the first thing she did was check her answering machine. Disappointment hit her when she saw the steady red light. It meant Jeff hadn't called while she was out. Damn! What was she thinking? She didn't want to talk to him.

But she did. Despite what had happened, despite her certainty that he was only grateful to her, she still wanted him. She still loved him and she missed him terribly.

Determinedly she made herself a cup of tea and then sat down to work on her files. But she couldn't concentrate; she kept remembering Jeff's words—"I love you and I want to marry you."

Then Mary's words would chime in from nowhere. "If you care about someone, you've got to take a few risks."

Over and over the words replayed themselves in her mind. A strange tension began to build in her. Throwing her pencil down, she stared into space for a long time.

Her emotions whirled in a tangle of confusion. Love meant taking risks; love meant believing and trusting. Love wasn't contingent on a tie of blood. Love didn't relegate a relationship from Friday nights to Sunday evenings.

The sun was setting when she reached for her purse. She dug out a phone number and stared at it blankly for a few moments before picking up the phone. Hannah didn't let herself think or feel as the phone rang five hundred miles away.

"Hello." The woman's voice was soft.

Hannah took a deep breath. "Hello, is this Irene Kenyon?"

"Yes?"

"This is Hannah Breckenridge. I'd like to see you."

Chapter Fourteen

Hannah stared out the window as the taxi pulled up to the curb in front of a three-story blue-and-white Victorian house. She paid the driver, got out and started slowly up the walkway.

She wasn't sure of her motives for coming. Maybe she was here because of Jeff, or maybe she was here for herself. All she knew for certain was that she was here now and there was no going back.

Taking a deep breath, she climbed the steps and crossed the porch. She was reaching for the brass knocker when the door swung open.

"Hello, Hannah." Irene smiled shyly. "I was waiting for you. I saw the cab pull up. Please come in."

Hannah stared at the woman who'd given her life. Dressed in a peach cable-knit sweater and matching knit skirt, Irene Kenyon looked both elegant and casual. Her short ash-blond hair was styled back and off her face, her makeup was subdued and flattering, and the small gold hoops dangling from her ears looked expensive.

She opened the door wider and Hannah quickly stepped inside, murmuring a polite "Thank you."

Irene led her across a parquet floor and into a graceful lilac-and-cream living room. "Please sit down." She motioned toward a flowered-chintz love seat. "Jeff told me you liked tea, so I've prepared some. I hope that's all right."

"That's fine," Hannah said quickly, sinking down onto the couch. On the glass-topped coffee table in front of her, there was a delicate white china tea service. Next to that was a tray of dainty pastries. "It was nice of you to go to so much trouble."

"It was no trouble at all," Irene murmured. She sat down in a matching wing chair opposite the coffee table. The two women studied each other from across the small space.

Hannah had no idea what to do. She suspected that Irene didn't, either. God knows, this situation certainly wasn't covered in most etiquette books.

"I'm so glad you came," Irene finally said. "I've wanted to meet you so badly. We all have."

"I know." Hannah bit her lip. "But I had my reasons for staying away." She shifted nervously.

Irene cleared her throat. "Yes, I expect you did. Well—" she rose to her feet "—let me pour you some tea. Do you take cream and sugar?"

"Yes. Both." Hannah relaxed fractionally as she watched Irene pour the tea. "How's Kirsten?" she asked.

Irene smiled broadly. "She's making great progress. They're going to let her come home next week. The doctor says if she keeps improving she can go back to school in September for her senior year." She placed the tea in front of Hannah.

"That's wonderful." Hannah smiled for the first time. "I'm so glad."

"It's all because of you, you know," Irene said. She sat down and regarded Hannah gravely. "We owe you more than we can ever repay. You saved my daughter's life."

A tiny pang went through Hannah and she hastily averted her eyes from Irene's compelling gaze. She didn't know what to say anymore. She was glad that Kirsten was going to make it, but she hated to take the credit. "You should really be thanking Jeff," she said quietly. "He's the one responsible. He's the one who found me. All I did was donate a little bone marrow."

"That's not all you did. You fell in love with him, didn't you?"

Hannah's head snapped up in surprise. Irene was watching her carefully. "Yes," she confessed, unsure why she felt compelled to be so honest, but determined to do it anyway. She was tired of lies. "I'm in love with him. I think that's the reason I'm here."

Irene sighed. "Did Jeff force you to come?"

"No," Hannah answered truthfully. "He did give me a push, but I think I would have wanted to meet you sooner or later, anyway." Hannah surprised herself by the admission. But it was true, nonetheless. Eventually even without the confrontation with Jeff, she knew she'd have to come to terms with herself and wanted to meet Irene. In one sense, Jeff had been right when he'd told her all those weeks ago that circumstances changed you.

She picked up her teacup and traced the rim with her finger. "I want to know—" she swallowed the lump in her throat and looked Irene directly in the eyes "—why you gave me away."

Irene closed her eyes briefly. "I was seventeen years old and flat broke. My parents, you see, threw me out when I told them I was pregnant."

Hannah's hand began to tremble so badly she had to put her cup down. "You must have been scared to death. Couldn't my father have helped you?"

"I was scared, all right." Irene smiled bitterly and sat back against the cushions. "Your father was only eighteen—just a boy. I conceived you the night before he left for the army. We were both from very poor families. Back in those days, the army was one way out of poverty for young men. I thought he loved me, but when I wrote and told him I was pregnant, he told me to get lost and claimed the baby wasn't his." She shrugged. "I had some money saved—enough for a bus ticket to Los Angeles, at any rate. We lived in a little town near the California-Oregon border and the only thing on my mind at the time was getting as far away as I could."

"I think I can understand that," Hannah said softly.

Irene rose and moved to sit next to her on the couch. "When I got to Los Angeles I managed to find a job and a room." She looked away. "I never planned to give you up," she whispered, "but after what happened, I had no choice."

Puzzled, Hannah asked, "What did happen? You had a job and place to live."

Irene shook her head. "But with medical costs and everything, I didn't have very much left after I had you. After I'd brought you home from the hospital, I realized my savings weren't going to last very long."

"You didn't give me up at birth?" Hannah was stunned. She'd always assumed Sam and Mary had taken her right from the hospital.

"No. But things went wrong almost from the very first—" Her voice broke and she clenched her hands. "You got sick when you were three weeks old. It was cold that winter. Cold and wet. Our room was damp and musty. I spent what little money I had taking you to the doctor, but you didn't get any better. Finally I was out of money, out of food and the landlord was threatening to put us on the street. I was sick by that time, too." Irene stared blankly at the wall as though she were reliving that terrible winter. A tear trickled down her cheek but she didn't notice. "Your breathing got erratic that night. You had pneumonia. We both did. I ran next door to a neighbor. Mr. Zimmer took us both to County General. By the time they admitted us, my temperature was 104 and you were burning up with fever, too."

Hannah felt tears well in her own eyes. But they weren't for herself. They were for the anguished young girl of twenty-nine years before. "Go on," she prompted gently.

"By the time I was well enough to be able to think, I realized I had almost killed you. I loved you so much, and I had almost let you die."

"But you didn't do anything wrong." Hannah surprised herself by defending the woman she'd always resented.

"That doesn't matter," Irene stated flatly. "You still almost died and it would have been my fault. I had no money, no education and no way to support you. I knew I couldn't keep you, no matter how much I wanted to. The staff at the hospital put me in touch with a social worker and I arranged for you to be adopted." Her voice trailed off and dropped to a husky whisper. Her elegantly manicured hand covered her mouth as though muffling the words would make them less painful. "The last time I saw you, you were a month old. You were in the arms of a petite blond woman who was smiling from ear to ear as she carried you to the elevator."

Irene closed her eyes at the memory. "I remember praying to God that she would love you as much as I did."

"She did," Hannah whispered tearfully. "Believe me, she did." She sat rooted to the spot, afraid that if she moved she'd shatter inside. She felt such pity for the young girl Irene had been trapped by brutal circumstances that forced her to give up her own flesh and blood.

"Hannah," Irene prodded gently "are you all right?"

"All right?" Hannah repeated dully. She drew herself up straight and flattened her hands against her thighs. "I don't know," she answered honestly, her voice reedy and thin. "I don't know what I'm supposed to feel."

"There hasn't been a day since you were born that I haven't thought of you, that I haven't loved you. Then, when your bone marrow saved your sister's life, I knew fate had given me a second chance. I had to see you. I'll understand if you hate me or if you don't want to have anything to do with me, but don't let your feelings about me keep you from loving my son."

"Jeff?" Hannah asked, thrown off balance.

Irene swiped at her cheeks and smiled. "He cares for you, Hannah. Even with Kirsten's almost miraculous improvement... he's been miserable this past week."

The wall inside Hannah crumbled and emotions washed over her like water from a bursting dam. She was caught in a conflict of hope and fear so intense that it made her tremble and gasp for air. "I love him, too," she managed to say before adding hesitantly, "And I don't hate you."

Overcome, Irene could do nothing but reach for Hannah's hand and cling to it. She began to cry quietly.

Hannah squeezed her eyes shut and gulped in several long, ragged breaths. For several moments, the two women sat huddled close together, each of them fighting to end their own internal battles of pain, loss and regret.

Shivering, Hannah drew herself up and gazed off into the distance. She didn't hate Irene; she didn't hate anyone. The anguish she'd been living with all these years drained away as the seconds ticked by, leaving in its place the sure knowledge that she had been well and truly loved her entire life. Her natural mother had loved her, her adoptive parents had loved her, and now she could only hope and pray that Jeff loved her, too. If it wasn't too late.

"Did Jeff tell you about us?" Hannah asked shyly. She drew back and looked at Irene.

"Not in so many words. But I guessed," Irene answered, giving Hannah's hand a gentle squeeze.

Slowly Hannah forced her rigid muscles to relax. She bit her lip as a shaft of uncertainty speared through her. "I don't think he cares anymore. I think I hurt him too much."

"There's only one way to find out," Irene said with a wise smile.

"You mean call him?"

"No, I mean go see him."

"But he's at work now."

Irene cocked her head to one side and grinned. "Well, you could come to the hospital with me now and meet Kirsten." She tried to keep her invitation casual and light, but she couldn't conceal the hope in her eyes. "That'll take a few hours." Her lips curved in a sly smile. "I have a key to Jeff's apartment and you could take that and wait for him there."

Hannah's heart pounded. If she said yes, she was agreeing to more than just a meeting with her half sister, and she knew it. If she met Kirsten, she'd never be able to walk away. But it was already too late; she realized that. From the moment she'd called Irene and asked to meet her, she'd taken the first step to having a relationship with her birth family. If she was wrong—if Jeff really was only feeling grateful—she'd be trapped in a relationship with her birth family that had the potential to make her miserable for the rest of her life. It was a risk and big one, but she was going to take it. Jeff was worth it. "I think that's a wonderful idea."

The two women smiled at each other like two strangers who'd suddenly found a common bond.

On the way to Jeff's apartment later that day, Hannah sagged back against her seat in the taxi. Sudden uncertainty swamped her.

She prayed silently. I hope I'm doing the right thing. I hope he still wants me. Maybe I should have called his office first, and told him I was coming. A loud blast from the cab's horn shook her out of her reverie. She straightened and got a grip on her spinning emotions.

That last night, he'd said he'd be waiting. Or did he say he'd come running? Hannah couldn't remember his words—only the promise behind them. She only hoped to God he'd really meant them. Firmly she clamped down on her doubts and pushed her fears to the back of her mind. Whatever happened tonight, she had to go to him. God knows, he'd come to her enough times.

She stared thoughtfully out the window. The taxi pulled up to a red light beside an old car filled with teenage girls. They were giggling and singing along to a rock tune blaring from the open window. Hannah grinned. They were about the same age as her sister.

She cast her mind back a few hours and sighed happily. The meeting with Kirsten had gone off without a hitch. Hannah had been nervous as she trailed Irene into Kirsten's hospital room. Her half sister was lying on the bed watching television. . . .

Kirsten had looked up and grinned. "Hi, Mom. Did you bring me those tapes—" She broke off as she spotted Hannah. "Wow!" she exclaimed, bolting upright. "It's Hannah."

"Hello, Kirsten," Hannah replied with a flustered smile. "How did you know who I was?"

"Jeff told me all about you. He said you were tall, auburn-haired and gorgeous, and as we don't know anyone else who fits that description, it has to be you." She sank back onto the pillows, another grin on her face.

"How are you feeling today?" Irene asked, leading Hannah over to stand by Kirsten's bed.

Kirsten kept her gaze on Hannah. "Fine," she responded cheerfully. "And now that *she*'s here, I'm feeling even better." She reached down and patted the bed. "Sit down and let's talk."

Hannah looked worriedly at Irene. "I don't want to get germs on you."

"Don't sweat it. Thanks to you, my WBC count is just fine. Come on, I've been wanting to meet you so much."

Irene nodded and pulled up a chair as Hannah perched on the side of the bed. "I've wanted to meet you, too," Hannah admitted with a shy smile. "I'm sorry it took me so long to get here."

"Ah, forget it," said Kirsten with a shrug. "Believe me, once you've coped with cancer you don't waste a lot of time worrying about petty stuff. You're here now, and that's all that's important."

Surprised by Kirsten's matter-of-fact attitude, Hannah glanced at Irene for guidance. Irene rolled her eyes heavenward. "I told you she was blunt."

"I just call 'em like I see 'em," Kirsten said nonchalantly. "Are you going to marry my brother?" she asked Hannah.

"Kirsten!" Irene scolded. "That's none of your business." She looked at Hannah helplessly. "I forgot to mention she's outrageous, too."

"It's okay," Hannah said with a laugh. She sobered and turned her head to look at Kirsten. "I'm going to marry him if he'll still have me," she answered softly.

"Don't worry about that," Kirsten said reassuringly. "He'll still have you. Jeff's sure been grumpy since he got back last Sunday. You two must have had a doozy of a fight. What was he doing? Trying to tell you what to do? You'll have to watch that man—he can be awfully bossy."

"Kirsten!" Irene yelped. "Mind your manners. For goodness sake, you're going to scare Hannah back to Southern California if you don't stop saying such rude things about your brother."

Kirsten looked totally unrepentant. Hannah broke into helpless laughter. "Jeff wasn't exactly trying to boss me around," she said with a rueful smile at Irene. "It was more like he was giving me an incentive to do the right thing."

Irene's face softened and a quiet message of understanding and acceptance silently passed between the two women.

As Hannah and Irene rose to leave an hour later, Kirsten grabbed her sister's hand.

"I never got a chance to thank you," she said seriously. "You know, for being my donor. You saved my life."

A great wave of tenderness washed over Hannah as she stared into her sister's wide, luminous eyes. She wondered why she'd been such a fool and waited so long before finding the courage to come here. "You don't have to thank me," she replied with a shaky smile. Impulsively she leaned down and kissed Kirsten's cheek. "I was glad to do it. After all, that's what families are for...."

After the taxi dropped her off in front of Jeff's apartment, Hannah looked around for his car. But the sporty black sedan wasn't parked in its usual spot and she couldn't see it anywhere else on the street.

She dug the key Irene had given her out of her purse and walked quickly toward the door before her nerve completely deserted her.

Jeff frowned as he got out of the elevator and stepped into the hall. Despite the luxurious cream-colored carpet and ivory walls, the passageway was dim and depressing. The shadowy interior did nothing to lift his downcast mood. He glanced up at the light fixture overhead. Two of the bulbs had burned out.

Slowly he walked to his apartment, putting off for as long as possible going inside and facing another endless, lonely evening waiting for the phone to ring. He was beginning to think it never would. Maybe he'd scared Hannah off for good.

His frown turned into an ominous scowl as he reached his apartment and saw a tiny shaft of light under his front door. Damn! he thought angrily. She's got me so twisted up inside I can't even remember to turn lights off. Shaking his head in disgust, he dug into his suit pocket for his key.

Nothing was right anymore. Absolutely nothing. The only bright spot in his life was his sister's almost phenomenal improvement. But even that joy wasn't enough to blot out the pain clawing at his insides and ripping him to shreds. He shoved the door open and stepped inside.

From a few feet away, Hannah came and stood in front of him. "Hello, Jeff."

Almost afraid to believe his eyes, he stopped and stared at her. His mind went blank and without his realizing it, so did his face.

She panicked at the utter lack of feeling she saw in his expression. Fear surged through her in a paralyzing rush. "Jeff..." She trailed off, afraid her voice would crack and she'd start to cry.

"Hello, Hannah." There wasn't a shred of emotion in his voice and her heart plummeted to her toes. "What are you doing here?"

"I came to see you." She stepped closer, hoping he'd take her into his arms. But he didn't move; he stood perfectly still and looked at her as if she were a ghost. "I went to see Irene and Kirsten," she said, and then cringed at the hopeful note in her voice.

She was afraid to breathe, to move, to do anything but stand motionless in front of him and see if it was really too late. Her pulse roared in her ears and she could feel the blood draining from her face.

He watched her for a long moment and then a slow smile spread across his face. "I'm glad you changed your mind," he muttered, pulling her into his arms and crushing her against his chest. Joy swept through him in a dizzying rush. He knew what this meant. He knew the kind of emotional risk she'd taken for him and he was simultaneously humbled and proud. Hannah was telling him in the only way she could that she believed in him, that she was willing to give him all of herself.

He picked her up and twirled her around. "Thank God," he muttered over and over as he spun her into the center of the room. "I was almost at the breaking point."

"Does that mean you'd have given in and called me?" she asked as he slowly lowered her to the floor. Her eyes were bright with tears of happiness.

"Yeah," he said, his voice rough with emotion. "I was going to give you another week to come to your senses." He crushed her to him again and took her mouth in a long, lingering kiss.

When he pulled away, his eyes were glittering with emotion and his expression was solemn. "We belong together, Hannah," he said in a gritty, rough voice. "I was beginning to realize that even if you couldn't bring yourself to meet Irene and Kirsten, even if you only wanted me for a part-time lover, I'd take it. I just couldn't forget you. You're too deeply imbedded in my soul. I'd have found a way for us to make it some-how."

"You don't have to now," she whispered softly, lifting her hand to stroke the taut muscles of his cheek. "Everything's going to be just fine. I'm not scared anymore. There'll be no more holding back. I believe in you and in your love."

He looked at her for a long moment and then he grinned. "Does that mean you want to be roomies again?" he asked hopefully.

"I think I'd like to be roomies again," she answered with a tiny smile. "This time, for good. That is, if you still want me."

Jeff let out a whoop of joy and swept her up again. "I love you, Hannah Breckenridge."

"I love you, too, Jeff Kenyon." She twined her arms around his neck and kissed his throat.

"I think I'd better make an honest woman of you soon," he murmured softly as she melted against him.

"Why?" she asked. She brushed her tongue over the sensitive skin at the base of his neck. He shuddered in response. "But if that's a marriage proposal, the answer's yes."

He laughed. "Because you're a preacher's daughter and I'm going to have my wicked way with you again. Right now." Bending slightly, he lifted her into his arms and strode to the bedroom.

As he laid her on the bed, his eyes grew serious. She was so perfect, so beautiful, so loving—and she was finally his.

Epilogue

"I tell you, Irene, that daughter of ours is going to drive me to drink." Mary tapped Irene gently on the shoulders. "Just look at her, stuffing that hot dog into her mouth. It's a good thing Jeff isn't here yet. He'd have a fit. The doctor warned her about too much salt."

Irene watched as Hannah cheerfully popped the last bite into her mouth. She sighed. "This pregnancy has turned her into a salt addict."

Hannah grinned crookedly at the two women sitting beside her on the bleachers. "Hey," she said, "it was just one hot dog. The doctor didn't say I had to give up salt completely. Besides, we're supposed to be celebrating. This is the homecoming game."

"Humph," Mary sniffed. "You think everything's a celebration. You celebrated when Kirsten went back to school, you celebrated when Kirsten made the cheerleading squad, you—" She broke off sheepishly as she saw the Kenyons and her own husband grinning from ear to ear. "Oh, well," Mary muttered, patting Hannah's slightly rounded tummy. "I guess you're right. One hot dog isn't going to hurt the baby."

Hannah's surprise pregnancy had been a happy accident. Four months after she and Jeff were married, she found herself pregnant—much to the delight of both families. Kirsten was over the moon at the thought of being an aunt.

Hannah laughed and gave Mary a quick hug. "Face it, you fraud," she whispered into her mother's ear. "You were whooping it up right along with me every step of the way. You're as tickled as I am about Kirsten's progress."

Mary giggled. "Okay, okay, I give in.... Oh, look! There she is." She stood up to get a better view as the cheerleading squad raced onto the football field in front to the team. A wild cheer went up from the crowd. This was the last game of the season and Kirsten's high school was tied for first place.

"Oh, isn't she cute in that little skirt! Oh, John—" Mary turned to her husband and nudged him in the ribs "—look at those yellow pom-poms. And Kirsten's hair... it's darling."

They were all on their feet now. Hannah looked around for Jeff then smiled as she spotted him coming out of the tunnel at the far end. "There's Jeff."

"Oh, good," Irene said. "I'm glad he made it on time." She turned to grin at Hannah. "Don't worry—" she dropped her voice to a conspiratorial whisper "—I won't mention the hot dog."

Hannah laughed again. Then she turned her attention to her sister and the rest of the cheerleaders as they took their spots. Kirsten was one of the lucky ones. She was going to make it. Her recovery was nothing short of miraculous.

Hannah glanced quickly around at the small, happy group and dabbed at her eyes. Irene and Mary were chatting excitedly, Reece and John were solemnly discussing the upcoming game, she was waiting for the man she loved, and her younger sister was having the time of her life. Sighing, she almost laughed out loud for the sheer joy of it.

"Hi, sweetheart." Jeff slipped an arm around Hannah and squeezed her tightly. "Has the game started?"

"It's about to," she replied. Her eyes narrowed as she stared at her husband. He was grinning at her like a cat that had stolen the cream. "What are you up to? Just where did you have to go this morning on that mysterious little errand you refused to tell me about?"

"I had to pick something up," he said nonchalantly. His mouth twitched as he tried to keep from smiling.

"What?"

"These." He held up two airline tickets. "For us. A trip to Hawaii."

"Oh, my gosh!" Hannah threw her arms around him. "That's fabulous. But what's the occasion?"

Jeff leaned down and brushed his lips against hers. "Our honeymoon," he whispered huskily. "I decided we deserved a little time alone—for once. I want you all to myself."

Hannah laughed. Since their marriage they'd been surrounded by a loving crowd from both sides. They'd only had time for a very short honeymoon earlier, because Hannah had to get back and hire a replacement for herself at the community center before moving into Jeff's apartment.

"I love you," she said softly, twining her arms around his neck and staring into his eyes. "I never knew life could be this good."

He smiled. "Neither did I." He flattened his hand over her stomach. "We've got it all, now. Each other, our families, and soon we'll have our baby." Jeff's grin faded and his expression turned somber. "I love you, Hannah Leigh, and I'm going to spend the rest of my life showing you how much. You'll never have any doubts again, I promise you."

Hannah smiled. Jeff's love had given her the courage to face herself. All her doubts and fears and anxieties had long since been laid to rest. She reached over and pulled his head down for a kiss. "Darling," she whispered as they drew apart, "I stopped having doubts a long time ago."

* * * * *

presents

SONNY'S GIRLS

by Emilie Richards, Celeste Hamilton and Erica Spindler

They had been Sonny's girls, irresistibly drawn to the charismatic high school football hero. Ten years later, none could forget the night that changed their lives forever.

In July—
ALL THOSE YEARS AGO by Emilie Richards (SSE #684)
Meredith Robbins had left town in shame. Could she ever banish the past and reach for love again?

In August—
DON'T LOOK BACK by Celeste Hamilton (SSE #690)
Cyndi Saint was Sonny's steady. Ten years later, she remembered only his hurtful parting words....

In September—
LONGER THAN . . . by Erica Spindler (SSE #696)
Bubbly Jennifer Joyce was everybody's friend. But nobody knew the secret longings she felt for bad boy Ryder Hayes....

SSESG-1

Take 4 bestselling love stories FREE

Plus get a FREE surprise gift!

from Lindsay McKenna

Soar with Dana Coulter, Molly Rutledge and Maggie Donovan—
Lindsay McKenna's WOMEN OF GLORY. On land, sea or air, these
three Annapolis grads challenge danger head-on, risking life and limb
for the glory of their country—and for the men they love!

May: NO QUARTER GIVEN (SE #667) Dana Coulter is on the brink
of achieving her lifelong dream of flying—and of meeting the man who
would love to take her to new heights!

June: THE GAUNTLET (SE #673) Molly Rutledge is determined
to excel on her own merit, but Captain Cameron Sinclair is equally
determined to take gentle Molly under his wing....

July: UNDER FIRE (SE #679) Indomitable Maggie never thought
her career—or her heart—would come under fire. But all that changes
when she teams up with Lieutenant Wes Bishop!